I0761122

BY DEMI WINTERS

THE ASHEN SERIES

The Road of Bones

Kingdom of Claw

Roots of Darkness

Dawn of the North

ROOTS OF DARKNESS

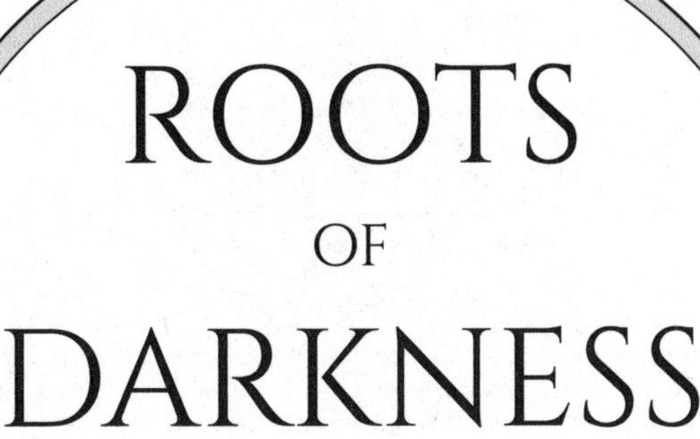

ROOTS OF DARKNESS

THE ASHEN SERIES
BOOK 2.5

DEMI WINTERS

DELACORTE PRESS | NEW YORK

Delacorte Press
An imprint of Random House
A division of Penguin Random House LLC
1745 Broadway, New York, NY 10019
randomhousebooks.com
penguinrandomhouse.com

Originally self-published in the United States by the author in 2025.

Hardcover ISBN 979-8-217-29983-6
Ebook ISBN 978-1-7389960-6-3

Printed in the United States of America

3rd Printing

First Delacorte Press Edition

Book Team: Production editor: Christa Guild • Managing editor: Saige Francis • Production manager: Meghan O'Leary • Proofreaders: Julie Ehlers, Laura Jorstad

Book design by Betty Lew
Jacket design and illustration by K. D. Ritchie at Story Wrappers
Map design by Megan Wyreweden

The authorized representative in the EU for product safety and compliance is Penguin Random House Ireland, Morrison Chambers, 32 Nassau Street, Dublin D02 YH68, Ireland. https://eu-contact.penguin.ie

TO EVERY WOMAN WHO'S HAD HER OPINION DISREGARDED BECAUSE SHE LACKS A CERTAIN APPENDAGE; WHO'S HAD HER PASSION BRUSHED OFF AND BEEN DEEMED "TEMPERAMENTAL"; WHO'S BEEN TOLD TO SMILE, AS THOUGH SHE NEEDS TO CHANGE HERSELF TO PUT OTHERS AT EASE.

I PUT ALL OF MY FEMININE RAGE INTO THIS ONE FOR YOU.

Author's Note

The Ashen Series takes place in a dark fantasy world and is intended for mature (18+) readers.

This book in particular deals with a domestic abuse survivor living with a disability (above-elbow amputation), has a scene depicting animal death, and includes explicit, open-door sex scenes.

A full list of content warnings is available at: https://demiwinters.com/trigger-warnings/

Please also note that a glossary and pronunciation guide are provided at the end of the book.

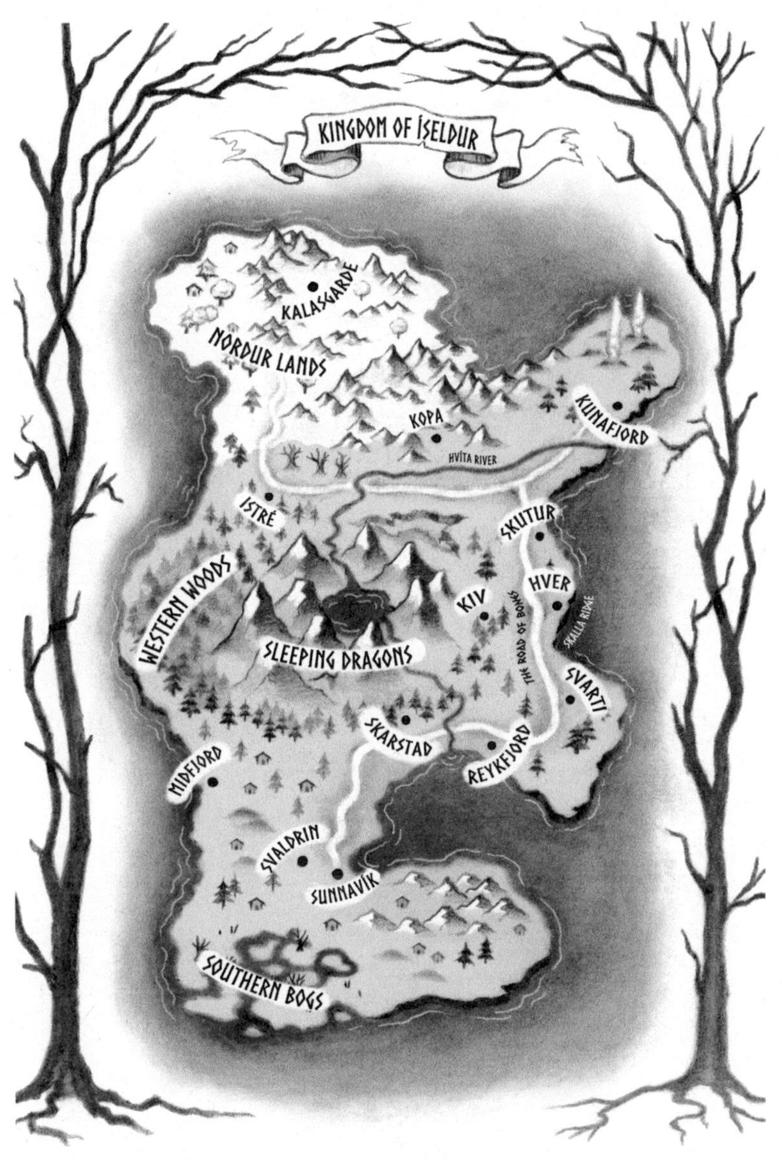

KINGDOM OF ÍSELDUR
KALASGARDE
NORDUR LANDS
KOPA
KUNAFJORD
HVÍTA RIVER
ISTRÉ
SKUTUR
WESTERN WOODS
HVER
KIV
SKALLA RIDGE
THE ROAD OF BONES
SLEEPING DRAGONS
SVARTI
SKARSTAD
REYKFJORD
MIDFJORD
SVALDRIN
SUNNAVÍK
SOUTHERN BOGS

Recap

Hekla "Rib Smasher" is a member of the Bloodaxe Crew, a group of viking mercenaries who specialize in hunting monsters. Other members of the crew include Reynir "Axe Eyes" Bjarg, and brothers Jonas "the Wolf" and Ilías "No Beard." After meeting with Magnus Hansson, King Ivar's chief hirdman, the Bloodaxe Crew sets off on a quest to reach the town of Istré and rid it of the deadly mist terrorizing its citizens.

According to reports, the mist has the sound of a beating heart; it emerges from the woods and leaves missing people in its wake. The Klaernar—King Ivar's specialized warriors—were sent to help. But the Klaernar's corpses were soon found secured to pillars with vines, and a symbol was written in blood, over and over.

In *The Road of Bones,* the Bloodaxe Crew leaves for Istré but soon discovers a stowaway in their wagon—Silla Nordvig, on the run after the queen's warriors killed her father. Though a secretive person, Silla integrates herself within the Bloodaxe Crew and becomes quick friends with Hekla. As a domestic abuse survivor, Hekla insists on teaching her self-defense.

But after the Bloodaxe Crew agrees to protect Silla from

the queen's warriors, Ilías "No Beard" falls in battle. Silla's lover, Jonas—the older brother of Ilías—feels betrayed. After drugging Silla, Jonas hands her over for a reward. Reynir "Axe Eyes" Bjarg, leader of the Bloodaxe Crew, goes to rescue her, leaving the Crew under Hekla's command.

In *Kingdom of Claw,* Rey is forced into hiding with Silla. He writes to inform Hekla that his old friend Eyvind Hakonsson will arrive with his retinue to help with the job. Now Hekla and the rest of the Crew—Gunnar and Sigrún—are in Istré, grappling with Ilías's death while trying to complete their task.

ROOTS OF DARKNESS

CHAPTER ONE

One week before the end of Kingdom of Claw
Istré

Hekla silently cursed herself as she peeled away from the warm firm body wrapped around hers. There was an art to extracting oneself from a bed companion—an art Hekla had never needed to learn. She had rules for dealing with her paramours, after all: No soft sentiments and no spending the night. But above all else, Hekla never allowed a man to have power over her.

Now she'd pay the price for breaking her rules. Hekla refused to consider how this man had convinced her to spend the night, not while contorting her body to slide out from under his heavy arm. Her bare feet hit the floor, and Hekla's chest swelled with victory. But the incoherent mutterings coming from the bed made panic spiral inside her. There was movement behind her, and Hekla braced herself for the man to awaken. But he simply rolled onto his back and stilled.

Releasing a long exhale, she slunk from the bed. Her first thought was that she was utterly naked and without her prosthetic arm. Her second was that brigands must have broken into the room. Bleary-eyed, she blinked at the chaos before her. A chair overturned near the hearth, fur rugs bunched and jumbled about.

The grandeur of her paramour's chambers was startling in the light of day. Between the twin hearths on either end of the room and the enormity of the bed in which her companion currently snored, she wondered how much such lodgings had cost him. But Hekla gave herself a mental shake and began the painstaking process of fishing her tunic and breeches from the detritus in the room. Where in the gods' sacred ashes had her arm gone?

Pulling her tunic over her head, Hekla tried to piece last night's events together. It had been the first of the Winter Nights, a celebration honoring the end of the harvest season, and the whole of Istré had gathered in the mead hall. Hekla had been in a sour mood. Her reasons were twofold: First, Istré's local chieftain had gone forward with the celebrations despite the threat of a murderous mist. And second, the blockhead had refused her participation in the festival's fighting games.

Instead, Hekla had watched Istré's locals stumble around the ring, knowing she could best them all while blindfolded. It had been a frustrating night indeed; that was, until she'd found an outlet for said frustrations.

Hekla glanced over her shoulder at the sleeping man. An assortment of shining black braids spilled across his angular cheekbones and jaw, his full lips buried in a neatly trimmed beard. A memory flashed in her mind of those lips pressing kisses up her sternum. She whipped away from him with a shaky breath and resumed searching for her missing arm.

She'd been reckless to lose track of it.

A sharp sound split the air, and Hekla's hand went instinctively to her dagger. It took her a moment to realize it was only the man's snores. He rolled once more, but she sensed he'd soon awaken.

Where was her gods-damned arm? She considered leaving without it. She could write to Axe Eyes. Have him arrange the production of a new one. The Tailor still had her measurements. Hekla could continue this job one-armed until a replacement was found.

It was at this moment that a gleam caught her eye—her arm, buried beneath a rug near the hearth. And with that, another unwelcome memory surged back. An expanse of golden skin as the man lay on that rug, clutching her hips while Hekla rode him . . .

She forced the thought aside and snatched her prosthesis before edging toward the door. Hand on the door latch, Hekla couldn't resist one last look toward the bed. But as she glanced his way, her companion's dark eyelashes fluttered.

With serpent-quick speed, Hekla dashed through the door. She didn't dare breathe until she reached her own chambers.

—∞∞—

"Open up, Fire Fist!" Hekla bellowed, pounding her left fist against Gunnar's door. "The crew from Kopa is here and we're to meet them this morning!" She paused, waiting for any sign of life in the room beyond. As expected, only silence met her ears.

With a sigh, Hekla rested her forehead against the door, sorrow and worry mingling within her. Ever since Ilías's death, Gunnar had been a shadow of himself, preferring to stay enclosed in his rooms. Hekla had done what she could to help him through his grief—had brought him food, drawn him baths, and even urged him to speak of his sorrows. And while she'd been content to pick up the slack so Gunnar could grieve in peace, today was different.

Hekla had returned to her chambers to find a note beneath her door. It seemed Eyvind bloody Hakonsson had arrived in Istré to take over the job with the mist, and he was three days early. Had Hekla known she'd be expected at the arse crack of dawn, she wouldn't have partaken in such late-night activities.

"Come on, Gunnar," Hekla pleaded, thunking her head against the door. "Let us go down for the daymeal. Meet Hakonsson and his men. Then you can return to your chambers."

A floorboard groaned, and the door cracked open, revealing Gunnar's tall, broad frame, clad in a rumpled tunic. His skin, normally a vibrant, deep brown, was ashen. New lines were carved beneath his eyes and into his brow. He looked, to put it mildly, like he'd aged a decade since Ilías's death.

Hekla schooled her face to hide her reaction.

"Let us get through this," said Gunnar blandly, closing the door behind him and pushing past Hekla.

With a relieved exhale, Hekla trailed behind him. She wished she could find the right thing to say to Gunnar—to bring back the jovial Fire Fist who loved puns and pocketing everyone's sólas at games of dice. But everything had changed since that day on the Road of Bones. They'd lost No Beard that day, the Wolf and Axe Eyes soon after. Never in a hundred years would Hekla have guessed *she'd* be holding the Bloodaxe Crew together in the absence of Axe Eyes.

For the hundredth time, she thought of the birch bark missive nailed to Istré's gates—the one with Rey's and Silla's likenesses etched upon it. *Slátrari,* it said, beneath Rey's face. Hekla had laughed it off at first. But as the days stretched on without Rey's arrival in Istré, she considered the facts. On the Road of Bones, Rey had shielded Silla from having to reveal the reason the Klaernar sought her. For a man who valued honesty above all else, it had seemed puzzling at the time. But now that Hekla considered it, wouldn't this out-of-character behavior make sense if Rey, too, were Galdra?

Galdra, perhaps, but the *Slátrari*? The murderer prowling the Road of Bones, burning people alive? That was entirely another matter. She wanted to look into his eyes and demand answers. But the knowing place inside Hekla told her to trust in his character. The Rey she knew was calculating. Strategic. And though he was gruff and cold on the surface, below that, Hekla knew he cared deeply for others. There was not a chance he'd murdered those people for fun; if he was, in fact, the Slátrari, there would be a good reason for the killings.

She sighed. The facts were what they were. Hekla had stepped in to fill Axe Eyes's role, and in the early days, she'd felt a sort of exhilaration. As a woman in a mercenary crew, she'd never thought such doors might be open to her. Though the circumstances were grim, she'd been eager to fill the role of leader of the Bloodaxe Crew.

That was until it became clear that Istré's chieftain had no interest in working with her. Loftur the All-Wise had brushed aside her every suggestion. In fact, the loathsome man barely tolerated her presence. It had been a shocking discovery for Hekla, who'd grown used to Rey's mindful consideration. He'd always allowed each member of the Bloodaxe Crew to voice their opinions.

Now Rey's friend from Kopa would arrive with his retinue to take control of the job, and Hekla found her eagerness rushing back. Perhaps this was the change they needed to convince Istré's hardheaded chieftain of what needed to be done. As Hekla and Gunnar descended the inn's stairs, she felt like a weary warrior, bolstered by an ally sweeping onto the battlefield at the last hour.

They passed through a short corridor into the adjacent mead hall. The Hungry Blade was quiet at this hour, candles flickering serenely in iron chandeliers, while morning light crept beneath the window coverings. But remnants of the previous night's celebrations were clear with the stale mead and sweat hanging in the air. The chaotic state of the room was a match to the chambers Hekla had recently vacated. She passed the slumped form of Onund Ale Drinker and winked at the exhausted-looking barkeep, Halldora, who hauled a kettle of róa across the room.

Sigrún seemed to materialize from thin air, touching Hekla's elbow gently. Light caught the scarred flesh climbing from beneath Sigrún's collar and across the side of her skull, her ash-blond hair flipped to the opposite side of her head, displaying the burns without shame.

Another memory jostled forth. Sigrún had been with her the night before, though only briefly. A group of strangers had entered the mead hall, and Sigrún had vanished into the shadows, not to be seen for the rest of the night. *Flighty* did not begin to describe Sigrún's behavior since Ilías's death. The petite warrior was as skittish as a squirrel.

"Are you well?" Hekla asked, signing the words as she spoke them.

Fine, Sigrún signed back, her gaze hard as she stared across the room.

Hekla followed her line of sight, gaze settling on the group of warriors seated at the far end of a long table. Their heads were bowed in quiet conversation, and Hekla felt a moment of apprehension. But she pushed it aside, reminding herself that these men were the reinforcements they badly needed. Shoulders back, she strode across the hall to greet them.

One voice lifted above the others, and Hekla's blood flamed hot in recognition. Loftur the so-called "All-Wise," village chieftain and official pain in her arse. Tall, with gray streaks in his blond beard, the man, Hekla guessed, had seen near fifty winters. Loftur lounged in the high chair like a king on his throne.

Hekla's smile turned brittle as she took in the warriors gathered around Loftur. All this time, she'd thought she could not get through to the man because she was not an Istré local. But as she watched him speak amiably with the warriors from Kopa, she suddenly understood.

Not a single pair of tits among them.

Feigning a casual air that she most certainly did not feel, Hekla strode across the mead hall, Gunnar and Sigrún flanking her.

"Ahh." Loftur's steely brown eyes met hers. "Here comes the Bloodaxe Crew now."

The warriors surrounding him shifted, watching her in silence.

Which one was Eyvind Hakonsson, trusted friend of Axe Eyes and a much-needed ally in her plight with Loftur? Hekla waited for one of the men to stand and introduce himself. But as they turned back to their róa in a less-than-warm welcome, Hekla scowled.

She knew nothing of this Eyvind, save that he was second heir to House Hakon. While everyone knew of Jarl Hakon, and his heir, Atli Hakonsson, Eyvind himself remained a mystery. She folded her arms over her chest, trying to quell her rising irritation. But then Hekla thought of Rey's letter—of how he'd vouched for Eyvind as a competent leader.

She opened her mouth to ask which of these men was Eyvind, but the mead hall doors banged open. The men at the long table shot to their feet, and Hekla turned to find two men striding into the hall. Squinting at the figures backlit by the intense morning light, Hekla's eyes fell first upon the stout man with an impressive, grizzled beard. He was dressed in the finest armor Hekla had ever seen, emblazoned with the dragon sigil belonging to House Hakon. But as her gaze flitted to the taller figure, a crimson cloak streaming behind him, her heart lurched.

She knew that cloak. "Ah, you're all here!" She knew that voice.

The figures approached, and Hekla felt the strangest sort of detachment—as though this was not happening before her very eyes.

But then, the inevitable happened: Their gazes locked. The man's hazel eyes widened only a fraction. Soft lips—lips she'd tried to forget—parted. He passed a hand over the intricate warrior braids woven along the sides of his skull—braids that Hekla had caressed the night before.

Her paramour recovered before she did. "Well met." He thrust a large hand out. "I'm Eyvind Hakonsson."

CHAPTER TWO

The Night Before

The sun crawled toward the horizon, the musky yet sweet scent of the harvest hanging in the air. The smell stirred a thousand memories within Hekla: her father's deep voice, singing the reaping song as he cut back the barley; her grandmother's stories as her crooked fingers worked the distaff. Hekla's family farm in Midfjord had been much farther south, the air less crisp than it was here in Istré. But the smell of the harvest was exactly the same.

Istré's beleaguered farmers would be reaping the barley this week before settling in for an uncertain winter. But tonight, at their chieftain's request, they'd gathered in the village square with the rest of the townsfolk.

Arms folded over her chest, Hekla observed the Winter Nights celebration. The dais at her back, with its three V-shaped pillars, was typically used for the Klaernar's executions. But now it hosted a group of grizzled warriors pounding a rhythmic beat on their drums. Braziers illuminated the whole of the square, including the hazel staves marking the borders of a fighting ring. Booths had been erected by vendors, the scent of flatbreads and roasted chicken drifting in the air. Horns of ale were passed about, and the crowd was in good cheer.

Hekla's head was already hazed with the ale she'd consumed in frustration at the Hungry Blade mead hall. This celebration was a mistake, but Loftur "the Unwise"—as she'd taken to calling him—refused to heed her warnings. It was bad enough the man blocked her every attempt to investigate the deadly mist stalking the outskirts of Istré. But watching these people celebrate the Winter Nights with such danger lurking nearby did not sit right with her.

There had been no sign of the mist tonight, but Hekla glanced at Istré's stockade walls, her nerves buzzing. She ought to have kept a clear mind, yet weeks of frustrations had frothed inside her. And Halldora, barmaid at the Hungry Blade, had been no help.

"You deserve some fun," she'd said with a wink, pressing horn after horn of ale into Hekla's hand. Hekla suspected the ale was a show of gratitude from Halldora. Upon her arrival in Istré, Hekla had immediately spotted the telltale bruises on Halldora's cheek. When at last she'd managed to corner the barmaid in private, Hekla had passed her a bag filled with coins.

"Bury it somewhere safe. And if ever the time feels right to leave him, you'll have a choice in the matter."

Halldora's dark eyes had brimmed with tears at the gesture, and Hekla had been unable to reveal it was what she'd once wished someone would do for her. It was more than coins. It was more than escape. It was acknowledgment. *I see you,* the bag said. *I understand.* Hekla wished she could do more—wished she could make true change in this kingdom to better the lives of women.

For now, she had to content herself with observing the fighting matches in Istré's town square, and gods, but they were difficult to watch. Alf the Slender succumbed to the sheer girth of Onund Ale Drinker, and he to the vise-like grip of Istré's blacksmith. Their fighting was messy and uncoordinated, any skill they might possess muddled by the vast quantities of ale they'd consumed. Hekla's limbs itched to leap into the ring, to show them how a true warrior fought. And perhaps she selfishly wanted to dispel Loftur of any preconceived notions he had of women in the fighting ring. But Hekla restrained herself. Betraying Loftur's orders would not win the man's favor. And so she reached for another horn of ale and downed it swiftly.

The blacksmith ambled from the ring, tipping a splash of his drink into the brazier's flames. Many of the locals had boldly made similar offerings—bits of chicken and beef, crudely carved weapons, and ale. Memory told Hekla such offerings were tailored to the old god Sunnvald's preferences, which had her scanning the crowd for tattooed faces. Should the King's Claws see such overt devotion to the old gods, Hekla suspected the monstrous mist would be the least of Istré's worries.

A new brawl was set to begin, the blacksmith against—

—a stranger.

Annoyance jostled through Hekla. To enter the tournament, one needed Loftur's approval. How had this newcomer gained entry into the games when she, who'd been trying for *weeks* to gain the blockhead's trust, was denied?

Hekla ground her teeth together, examining the stranger. Light from the brazier illuminated the man's pompous red cloak and cutting olive cheekbones. Some women might swoon over a pretty face like that, but Hekla liked a little grit to her men. To her surprise, as the stranger stepped into the fighting ring, she could tell each step was laced with power.

As the brawl began, Hekla could immediately tell the mysterious warrior held himself back. He let the blacksmith tackle him to the ground. Allowed him to land a few blows before rolling the blacksmith onto his stomach and wrapping an arm around his neck. The blacksmith pounded the ground, granting victory to the stranger, and the crowd roared. That was the precise moment that ale sloshed from her neighbor's cup right down the collar of Hekla's lébrynja jacket.

She'd officially seen enough.

Scowling, Hekla retreated from the festivities, the crowd's cheers chasing her through the darkened streets of Istré.

———

The night was clear and dark, stars spattered across the skies as Hekla laid a blanket down on the riverbank. Entering through barred culverts under Istré's defensive walls, the river snaked right through the town. This particular curve in the river was favored by locals for bathing, but given that every citizen was now gathered in the square, Hekla had it all to herself.

For a moment, she simply sat on the blanket, letting the

quiet of the night surround her. But soon the thoughts slunk out like wolves from the darkness. Why did Loftur block her every move? How could she convince him to work *with* her, rather than against her? Was it simply that she was a woman, or was there more to it?

Her questions shifted to irritation, and Hekla began to argue with the chieftain inside her head, trying to force logic into his thick skull. How could he expect the Bloodaxe Crew to defeat the deadly mist without being allowed to enter the woods, and why did he hold these infernal celebrations despite the ever-present threat? But even inside her mind, Loftur was as immovable as a mountain; no matter what she said or did, Hekla could not seem to get through to him. The man's refusal to listen was maddening!

The spilled ale on her neck was suddenly unbearable. Hekla shot to her feet and yanked off her lébrynja jacket. After tossing it on the riverbank, she moved to pull off her undertunic.

A twig snapped behind her.

Years of training had her drawing her blade without a heartbeat's hesitation. Hekla held still as death, eyes surveying the shadowed brush for any sign of movement. And after a moment, there it was.

There *he* was.

The stranger's red cloak drifted behind him as he ambled out of the bushes and onto the riverbank.

"This bank is taken," said Hekla, the point of her sword angled toward him. "Find another one, warrior."

Emotions played across his face—shock, then amusement, before settling into a look of haughty indignation.

"I think not," he said, strolling past her sword point, completely unbothered.

A week's worth of Loftur's disregard caught up to Hekla in a rush. It was one man too many brushing her aside when she could gut him like a fish. With a growl, Hekla charged after the man. Grabbing his shoulder, she whirled him around. Her sword tip now dimpled the tender skin of his throat.

"I said find another riverbank."

"And I," said the man, "*declined*."

She saw his tell—the flare of his pupils—but his speed caught her by surprise. As her sword was knocked aside, Hekla knew she was right. The man *had* been holding back in Istré's fighting ring. But her opponent did not know that Hekla had surprises of her own. She ducked, throwing her shoulder into his abdomen. His soft *oof* filled her with satisfaction as momentum carried the pair of them back toward a prickly willow bush.

Somehow, the warrior diverted their course, bringing them down on the soft riverbank instead. In a dizzying move, he twisted until Hekla's back hit the sand.

"And here I thought Istré would be dull," drawled the warrior from where he straddled her hips. "The first night and already I've a vixen beneath me."

"I'm no vixen, you braying ass," she spat. "Best you learn that."

Hekla brought her head crashing forward. The warrior reeled back in time to avoid a broken nose, but his distraction was enough for Hekla to wrench them sideways, rolling until the man was pinned beneath her.

Moonlight slanted across his tanned skin, and Hekla finally got a look at the man's eyes.

"Hazel," she muttered. "Of course." The man truly was obscenely pretty. Cheekbones that could cut glass. Glossy black hair, twisted into braids with such complexity it hurt her skull to even consider. And those eyes, trained on . . . she looked down, trying to determine what he was looking at. Her undertunic hung low, giving him a view straight down it.

"If your aim was to distract me, consider me distracted," he said, staring unabashedly at her breasts. The irritating man simply lay there, making no attempt to remove her from his body.

"Watch yourself, warrior," she growled. "I've anger to spend and have been looking for a target."

Those hazel eyes snapped to hers, then narrowed. "Why did you not join the games? You're more than an adequate opponent." His gaze drifted downward once more. "From what I can see."

With a huff, Hekla pushed off him and yanked her undertunic up.

"Fight me," said the warrior, hopping to his feet.

She surveyed him, left hand itching to pummel his pretty face. But now she knew he was a worthy opponent. Hekla thought of Axe Eyes—of how fiercely she missed their morning sparring sessions.

She eyed the warrior. There was no doubt he was one of the most handsome men she'd ever laid eyes upon, a fact that made her insides writhe in discomfort. Her husband, too, had been handsome, though it had only served as a tool to conceal his vileness. Hekla forced her gaze over his shoulder.

"What do you get out of it?"

"I get to fight a true opponent."

"Hmm. Not much enjoyment in holding back against Istré's citizens, is there?"

The man's eyes brightened. "The fact that you've a keen enough eye to notice tells me you'll be a worthy adversary." He reached for the buckle of his battle belt. It fell to the ground with a *thunk* that Hekla felt in the pit of her stomach.

She itched to do the same. Weeks stuck in this hovel; weeks with her every move shackled by Loftur; weeks without her sparring partner. Hekla had kept with her morning routines but felt herself slipping. She needed an opponent. Someone to give her the challenge she craved.

"Very well," she said, reaching for her own belt.

CHAPTER THREE

Present Day

Hekla stared at Eyvind Hakonsson's outstretched hand, blood roaring in her ears. How could she not have realized—that ridiculous red cloak, the elaborate, fussy braids, the splendor of his lodgings—it all seemed so obvious now. Gods, she was careless to have thrown out all her rules—to think that she might have a moment's freedom without consequences.

But a new thought had panic rising inside her. What if he revealed how they knew each other? Hekla's reputation would be irreparably damaged. No warrior at that table would respect her after discovering she'd taken their leader to bed.

Gunnar's elbow landed sharply in Hekla's ribs, spurring her into motion. She slid her left hand into his and shook it vigorously.

"You're early," she muttered.

Eyvind Hakonsson blinked then chuckled softly. The sound spurred memories of riverbank silt and slick skin—of frantic hands and feverish mouths.

"You're Hekla," he said, yanking her back to the present. It was more than a statement. It was, unmistakably, a discovery.

A man beside Eyvind cleared his throat, and they both turned toward him.

"Meet Konal, my adviser," said Eyvind, gesturing to the man.

Hekla forced her attention to Konal. He was dressed in House Hakon finery, his face lined with age, his beard streaked with gray. But Konal's eyes had a cunning look to them, and as he studied her, Hekla had the distinct impression he'd measured her worth and found her lacking.

As Konal and Eyvind's attention turned to Gunnar and Sigrún, Hekla tried to corral her nausea. Eyvind hadn't revealed their acquaintance with each other, and if her fortune held, he would not. *Get ahold of yourself,* she thought. *You must not show weakness before these warriors.*

Eyvind gestured for the warriors to take their seats, and Hekla found hers beside Gunnar. She reached for a jug of róa, but a hand landed on her shoulder. She whirled to face him.

The Fox.

In the light of day, his face was still beautiful. *I've seen you naked,* his amused expression seemed to convey. Was he waiting for the perfect moment to reveal it to the whole of his retinue? Make her the butt of some joke?

At the very thought of it, Hekla felt vulnerable and small—a feeling she'd not had since she'd been married. Hadn't she vowed to never feel that way again? How could she have discarded her rules, her defenses?

Anger surged forth, and Hekla readied herself to extend her claws. But Eyvind, reading something in her face, cleared his throat and wisely stepped back.

"Stand and tell us what you know, *Hekla,*" he said, all traces of amusement gone as he assumed the role of leader. "Bring us up to date on your findings."

As Hakonsson retreated to a seat of honor, Hekla could finally breathe. She pushed to her feet and smoothed down the leather-like scales of her lébrynja jacket.

"We've observed the mist from atop Istré's walls twice since our arrival," Hekla began. "It begins with a low, steady sound, much like a beating heart, yet this sound remains distant, somewhere in the woods, even when the mist emerges. Thus far, the mist can travel roughly fifty paces from the edge of the forest. At that point, it seems to lose power."

"Power?"

Hekla's gaze met Eyvind's, and she felt it right down to her toes. But with each word, Hekla became more grounded in herself—in her purpose. She was damned good at her job, and these were her allies.

"The mist . . . scatters, for lack of a better term, much like fog under bright sunlight."

Eyvind's thick brows drew together as he puzzled over this new detail.

"Loftur has ordered the local woodsmen to fell the trees bordering Istré," said Hekla, sending the chieftain a begrudging look of approval. "There is now a clearing of roughly one hundred paces around Istré's fortifications, though it must be noted that there are countless farmsteads beyond the walls still lacking protection—"

"Is there a pattern to the attacks?"

The interruption came from the man seated beside her. With striking blue eyes set against medium-brown skin, the warrior had a haughty expression she immediately disliked.

"There . . . appears to be a pattern," admitted Hekla. "Though we've made little sense of it. The mist appears roughly twice a month, always at night, but the timing between the incidents is always shifting. Thus far, the mist has engulfed three farmsteads along the borderlands. We've investigated all but one."

The hall was silent, so she forced herself to continue. "The Bloodaxe Crew has examined the steadings, measured the claw marks, and collected samples of the blood left behind, but we must see the first steading, must venture—"

Konal cleared his throat, setting Hekla's nerves on edge.

"Tell us about the murdered Klaernar," said Eyvind smoothly.

It did not go unnoticed that twice now the conversation had been diverted from Loftur's shortcomings. Hekla glanced among the three men in seats of honor, trying to understand. She'd hoped to find a sympathetic ear from Eyvind Hakonsson, but his familiarity with Loftur left her off-kilter.

"King Ivar ordered a squadron of Klaernar to Istré to aid in the investigation," Hekla continued. "The entire squadron was found not two days after their arrival, strung to the pillars in Istré's town square, secured by what appeared to be vines."

"How were they killed?" Konal asked, looking to Loftur.

Hekla bit her tongue to let Istré's chieftain answer.

"The puncture wounds were round," answered Loftur,

"and of similar size to the vines. Spiral Staves were scrawled in blood all around them."

The hall was silent as Eyvind and his men took in this information.

When Hekla could stand it no longer, she continued, "We spoke of this oddity often during our journey north. Axe Eyes and"—she sighed—"the rest of the Bloodaxe Crew were in agreement that it was likely a different perpetrator than the mist."

Eyvind and Konal exchanged a weighted look, and the men seated at the long table whispered among themselves. Her dismay was growing with each passing minute as she felt herself losing their attention. Why was it so gods-damned hard for a man to hear her words?

Hekla folded her arms over her chest. "We ought to speak of the creatures seen emerging from the woods!" she called out. As the room quieted, she continued, "The creatures we've seen are not as they were made. Foxes, grimwolves, wolfspiders alike. All of them carry a distinctive moldered scent, and their eyes burn like the embers of a fire." Her gaze landed on Loftur and hardened. "I've suggested it might be an illness born of the mist. Yet if that were so, I question why we've yet to find a single human survivor. The residents of the steadings impacted by the mist have all vanished, though the blood and claw marks suggest they've met a grim fate—"

Konal grunted, and Eyvind pushed to his feet. "My thanks, Hekla," said Hakonsson. "You may take a seat."

His casual dismissal landed like a slap. Hekla sank onto the bench, trying to quell her rising anger.

"After conferring with Loftur and Konal," said Eyvind Hakonsson, standing at the head of the table, "it has been decided. Today we shall ride beyond Istré's walls. Examine the site of the second attack—"

"We've examined it already," Hekla cut in. "As we have the site of the third attack. What we need is to visit the site of the first attack. The Hagensson steading."

Konal sent her a glare that could shatter stone, but Hekla stood her ground.

"As I've told you many times," Loftur said through clenched teeth, "the Hagensson steading has had a ritual cleansing. It must be left undisturbed for a full year to allow the dead to rest."

Loftur had explained to her that they'd originally thought the culprits behind the Hagenssons' disappearance to be rogue outlaws, and as such, a ritual cleansing had been performed. Once they understood the true scope of the problem and had sent word to King Ivar, Loftur had been instructed to leave the other affected steadings so the king's investigators could examine them. But Hekla couldn't shake the unsettling feeling there was something at that first steading Loftur didn't want her to see.

"As I was saying," Eyvind said, a note of irritation in his voice as his gaze flitted to Hekla for the barest of moments, "today we shall examine the site of the second attack. The Braksson steading."

"Perhaps while we're there," Hekla said, fighting to control her breaths, "at the very least, we can examine the inner border of the Western Woods."

Konal folded his arms across his barrel chest, and Hekla felt her hands flex. Gods, she'd known this man all of two minutes, and already she wanted to throttle him.

"Today," said Eyvind, in a disgustingly diplomatic voice, "we shall examine the *farmlands*. Nothing more." His warning gaze fell on Hekla. "We shall not enter the woods."

She eyed House Hakon's heir-in-waiting, trying to understand. Why did these men brush aside her every suggestion? Why did they not trust in her words and the work she'd invested into this job? She felt as though she were going mad. Were her suggestions truly so brash?

"We *must* go deeper," she tried. "Already, we've examined the farmlands and are no closer to understanding this mist. The time for caution has passed. Bolder action must be taken."

"As I've said before," said Loftur the Slow-Witted, "that is not an option."

Eyvind lifted a placating hand. "Loftur has explained his dilemma to me, and I believe a compromise can be found—"

Her patience snapped. "What is this dilemma, *All-Wise*?" Hekla's tone made it clear she found the man's name entirely unsuitable. "Your need to consume as much ale as you can while your people die?"

A sound of displeasure escaped Loftur. Beside him, an incredulous laugh burst from Eyvind, but he schooled himself as Hekla turned her glare upon him. She tried to find a single redeeming quality about the bootlicker before her. Where was the man she'd opened up to the night before?

As though reading her assessment, Eyvind's jaw flexed, a crack showing in his demeanor. "I do not know how Axe Eyes ran things," he said in a hard voice, "but I prefer to gather all information I can before rushing into danger."

Hekla battled the urge to scream in frustration, but it only grew stronger at the look exchanged between Loftur and Eyvind.

"What Loftur is about to share," said Eyvind, "is in strict confidence. If I hear it has left this room, I swear to you now, I will track down the perpetrators and cut the tongues from their mouths."

Loftur stood and hefted his belt up. "We in Istré have a long and complicated relationship with the Western Woods," he began. "Wardens, they once called us. Guardians of the woods. We honored the gods and the lesser spirits. But seventeen years ago, that all changed."

Loftur's gaze grew distant, and the unspoken words rang loud in the room: seventeen years ago, when the Urkans had invaded and outlawed worship of Íseldur's old gods. Hekla's gaze narrowed on Loftur as she wondered what nonsense this blockhead was about to spew.

"For seventeen years, we've forsaken our gods," continued Loftur. "Have abandoned our rituals and the old ways. Our link to this land has been weakened. And slowly, our gods, too, have abandoned us. The winters have grown long. The woods have grown wild. Unnatural creatures abound. And now, the mist."

Loftur stroked his long beard. "Sunnvald came to me in a dream."

Here we go, thought Hekla, battling the urge to roll her eyes.

"The Sun God told me that the mist is a sign of imbalance—

that to restore balance we must restore our broken faith. And so, it is Sunnvald's decree that we rekindle our weeklong Winter Nights celebrations, which culminate with a grand feast on the night of the double black moon. When Sunnvald is restored to His full strength, He will banish the mist and heal both our people and our lands."

Hekla glanced around the room, waiting for laughter or mockery, but she was greeted with silence. She exchanged an incredulous look with Sigrún.

Surely, they do not believe this nonsense? Hekla signed.

Sigrún shook her head, dumbfounded.

But Eyvind Hakonsson smiled broadly at Loftur. "I see no fault in these plans, Loftur," he said jovially. His gaze quickly found Hekla's, and it was clear his next words were meant for her. "It is important that we respect Loftur's wishes while we are in Istré. He's an old friend of my father's and comes from a long line of chieftains."

Hekla snapped her mouth shut before every thought in her skull could spill out. She stared at Eyvind, trying not to show her dismay. It was beginning to make sense. Eyvind's father was a friend to Loftur. He hadn't come to help the citizens of Istré at Rey's behest. He'd come with orders from his father to assist Loftur.

Eyvind looked out over his men. "Today marks the start of a new partnership. The Bloodaxe Crew joins forces with House Hakon." He looked to Loftur, nodding. "Together, we shall vanquish the mist and restore peace to Istré."

It took all of Hekla's energy not to storm from the hall. The man had ignored every word she'd spoken and had made promises that would be impossible to keep.

Your nose is wrinkling, signed Sigrún, and Hekla tried to relax her face.

"Let us take the daymeal together," continued Eyvind, gesturing to the long table.

Hekla bit down on a retort as Gunnar nudged her. "What happened to making a good first impression?"

She scowled at the table. First impression indeed. Their new leader was nothing but a hound on his father's leash. He'd just silenced her before a hall full of warriors. He was no ally of hers. She ought to march out of this mead hall. Send a missive to Axe Eyes at once. But as Halldora swirled up with a fresh kettle of róa, Hekla was reminded that the citizens of Istré were innocent in this. Someone had to protect them.

She drew a deep breath and gathered the information she had. Hekla did not know Axe Eyes's current location, and storming from the hall would only leave Istré in the hands of incompetents.

No. If she wanted to help the people of Istré, Hekla would have to play the games of these men and let them think they were winning.

CHAPTER FOUR

Hekla tapped her metal fingers against the mead hall's table, waiting as House Hakon's warriors extracted themselves from the benches and made their way to the yard out back. She itched to leave and join their morning sparring session, but Eyvind had asked her to stay behind. Based on the condescending looks his warriors had sent her, she was fairly certain she was about to be scolded.

Slowly, the warriors cleared out of the mead hall, Konal lingering so long, she thought he would stay. Hekla couldn't help but scowl at the man. Why in the eternal fucking fires did Eyvind Hakonsson need an adviser?

But Eyvind sent Konal a pointed look, and with a curt nod, the older man shuffled out back. And then they were alone. Hekla swiveled on the bench, folding her arms over her chest.

When first she'd discovered Eyvind's identity, Hekla had been knocked off balance, but now her feet were firmly planted on the ground. The way he'd disregarded her opinions, not to mention his obvious favoritism of Loftur, made Hekla eager for his suffering. She stared at Hakonsson expectantly, hoping to knock him askew—perhaps make him squirm a little.

But Eyvind did not have the good sense to look concerned in the least. He flopped onto the bench across from her and folded one leg over his knee. The gesture was maddeningly casual considering his treatment of her before his men. And then he had the audacity to smile. *Smile!*

"So," he said.

Hekla's glare intensified. "So . . . *what*?" she burst out, then chastised herself for letting him get under her skin.

His hazel eyes roamed her face. "Why did you sneak out this morning?" he said, just as Hekla blurted, "*This* is your second chance?"

A groove formed between his black brows, his gaze coming to rest on her mouth. Hekla's gods-damned heart kicked up a beat.

"Mistake," she muttered. "Last night was a mistake. Had I known who you were, I'd have put a stop to it."

Eyvind blinked as her words landed. He ran a hand along the side of his head, where neat rows of braids gleamed under torchlight. "I do not regret it," murmured Eyvind, meeting her gaze and holding it far too long for her liking. "How could I?"

"Spoken like a man," huffed Hekla.

"There were two of us on that riverbank, *Lynx,*" he said with a glint in his eye.

Hekla tried to ignore the roll of her stomach. "Of course you would not consider it," she snapped. "What would your men think of me should they discover I took you to my furs?" How did she explain to a man who'd been handed everything in life how hard she'd had to fight to get where she was now?

Eyvind's gaze grew distant as he pondered her words. "Aye, but you're right."

Shock bristled through her at this admission, but Hekla quickly schooled it from her expression.

"I can promise you, Hekla, I won't speak a word of it." Amusement was back, dancing in his eyes. "And as much as I'm tempted to repeat last night—"

Images of scarred golden skin and a poorly drawn dragon tattoo skimmed through her mind, but Hekla shoved them sternly aside.

"—we cannot," Eyvind concluded.

"That suits me just fine, Foxie," said Hekla, frowning as his eyes brightened at her use of that name. "Best we forget it ever happened."

"Yes," he said, his cunning smile widening. "Though it did. Happen."

Hekla pursed her lips, her insides heating through.

"Three? Four times?" prodded Eyvind, arrogant male pride shimmering in his gaze.

She scoffed, then looked away. "I suppose that's squared," Hekla muttered, making to stand.

"So we're clear," Eyvind said, and she could tell he was trying to rein himself in, "this job *must* go smoothly. It is a tremendous opportunity."

"Opportunity," repeated Hekla, all amusement draining from her. "For whom? Istré's citizens, who are being slaughtered?"

Eyvind leaned forward, bracing elbows on his knees. "Listen, Lynx," he said in that stern leader's voice. She felt the name right down to her toes.

Let me see how deep I can get, Lynx.

Hekla exhaled shakily.

"You cannot speak to me like that. Not before my men and especially not before Loftur and Konal."

"They're not here now, Hakonsson," she said roughly. "So I think I'll speak my piece. You want this job to go smoothly? It won't happen if you follow Loftur's deranged plan. We must visit the site of the first attack, and we *must* venture into the woods."

He shook his head. "Ever impatient, aren't you?" he murmured, and she made the mistake of locking eyes with the man.

No, Lynx, don't come for me yet.

To her great irritation, Hekla found her cheeks warming, and she forced her gaze away.

"Our orders are to appease Loftur. He's not the sort of man we can plow over."

"Orders?" said Hekla, with mock innocence. "Has there been a missive from Axe Eyes? I should like to see it."

Eyvind's gaze slid away as a muscle in his jaw feathered. "What I'm saying," he continued, "is that we must find a way to work with Loftur."

"I've tried working with him for *weeks,* Hakonsson," snapped Hekla. "The man's skull is filled with rocks!"

Those hazel eyes narrowed on her, and she felt him weighing this new version of her against the one he'd met last night. Combative and headstrong. Intolerant of fools.

"Try to exercise some self-restraint, Hekla." The man's commanding voice was threaded with amusement—a fact that made her blood simmer. "Give me a few days. See if I might soften Loftur to the idea of visiting the site of the first attack."

His words gave her pause. Perhaps Eyvind Hakonsson had some brains in his skull, because it sounded to Hekla like the meeting she'd just witnessed had been meant to appease Loftur. And yet, Eyvind was clearly the kind of man who enjoyed games of politics—who would use other people as pieces on his game board.

Instinct urged Hekla to fight back against such games, but what she'd been doing for weeks had gotten her nowhere. Perhaps it was best to keep an eye on Eyvind Hakonsson and see if he could gain any traction.

"Fine."

The corners of Eyvind's lips twitched. "That was hard for you, wasn't it?"

She sent him an irritated look.

"No more disrespect before my men."

Her brows lifted. "And alone?"

Eyvind fought against a smile. "If you must."

"Oh, I must."

He ran a large hand down his face in a poor attempt to conceal his glee. "You're going to make this difficult for me, aren't you?" At her casual shrug, he sighed. "I ought to have known you were *the* Hekla Rey wrote of—"

"What, precisely, did Axe Eyes say?" asked Hekla, spine stiffening.

"Only that you're one of the most competent warriors he's ever led."

"Not competent enough to lead this job, apparently."

His gaze grew contemplative. "Rey sent for me because

he needed someone who could . . . understand Loftur. Who can appease and flatter him, and"—Eyvind lost the battle to his smile—"I can see your talents are better suited for the battlefield."

"More likely, I do not have the right *equipment,*" quipped Hekla, jerking her head toward his groin. "I wager if I had one of those, Loftur would have listened to me now. The mist would probably already be vanquished."

"But you don't," said Eyvind, his smile deepening. "I know that for certain."

Her stomach rolled, and she cursed those gods-damned oatcakes for not sitting well.

"I can see you do not agree with my methods, Hekla. And I know you've weathered much in the past month. But we shall not accomplish anything if you continue to butt heads with Loftur. Join the team. Play your part. And eventually, we will sort out this mess."

With a pained sigh, Hekla nodded. At least she now knew Eyvind agreed with her assessment; the first steading needed to be examined, and they *must* scour the woods for clues.

"And," said Eyvind, "now that I know the damage our dalliance might do to your reputation, I'd like to assure you that I won't speak a word of it."

She opened her mouth to reply, but the door cracked open, Konal filling the frame.

"Eyvind," he said, his voice gruff. "I need a moment. Alone."

Ignoring the old warrior's hard gaze, Hekla pushed to her feet. "Well, Hakonsson, I suppose I shall go integrate myself into your retinue." She couldn't keep the cocky smirk from her face. "A shame I'll have to find myself a new sparring partner."

Eyvind's smile was back, those mischievous eyes like a hook in her belly, luring her in. Hekla hastily turned on her heel and strode from the hall as quickly as she could.

CHAPTER FIVE

The Night Before

Hekla's blood pumped hot with vigor as she squared off against the mysterious warrior. An hour they'd been at this. He was as adept as any warrior in the Bloodaxe Crew—quick and lithe, yet unpredictable. It was thrilling to find her own skill matched—to lose herself in the movements. And it was clear the warrior was enjoying himself, too; a bright smile gleamed from within his beard, hazel eyes catching the glow of the sister moons.

The warrior lunged, kicking out, and Hekla danced back just in time.

"You tried that once before," she teased.

"Mmm?" His smile broadened. "And this?" He dove at her, and this time, Hekla was too slow. He swept her feet out from beneath her, and she toppled backward onto the ground.

As her senses returned, the warrior straddled her, pinning her hips and shoulders down. Black braids spilled across his sweat-dampened brow, those hazel eyes glinting with mischief.

"Get off me, you lout!" Hekla bucked up, trying to dislodge the man, but all it did was create maddening friction where their bodies touched.

The warrior's fingers dug into her shoulders as something in his gaze shifted. It was confusion and discovery, like she was a mystery he was trying to untangle. For a moment, they stared at each other, the air between them growing charged. But then the irritating man's face broke into a grin that was far too victorious for Hekla's liking.

"Do you yield?"

Behind him, the river water rushed, and an idea formed in her mind. "Aye."

He lingered for a moment, then pushed to his feet and extended a large hand. Hekla slid her metal hand into his, eyes twinkling. With a deft twist, she unhooked her prosthesis from the joint anchored into her residual limb and gave it a shove. Surprise etched into the man's features, his mouth a wide O as he stumbled backward, clutching her detached arm. And then he vanished over the riverbank. Hekla leaped to her feet and ran to the embankment, cackling with glee at what she saw below.

The warrior floundered in the shallows. After regaining his balance, he stood, rivulets of water running down his face and plastering his tunic to his well-honed body. He shook his head like a dog, water flying from his black hair, and she couldn't keep her smile at bay.

"I see now," he said, shaking her metal arm. "You've many tricks . . . up your sleeve."

"I take my advantages where I can."

Hekla wiped the tears from her eyes as he strode from the

water. When had she last laughed like this? Weeks, at least. Not since Ilías's death.

The warrior placed her metal arm onto the grassy top of the riverbank, then climbed over it with a look of feral intensity. Hekla's stomach swooped low. And as he lunged at her, *perhaps* she was intentionally slow to respond. *Perhaps* she didn't fight as he hauled her over his shoulder. The warrior bounded into the river, plunging them both into the cold depths. As Hekla broke the surface, she was still laughing.

She pulled the tie securing her braid and used her fingers to loosen the strands.

The warrior watched her with keen interest. "You know," he drawled, "you're the first true challenge I've had tonight."

Hekla rolled her eyes. "Flattery will get you nowhere with me."

"And what will?"

Her gaze snapped to his, and she realized how near he stood. She watched a droplet of water run down his temple and disappear into his beard.

"Get me somewhere." He stepped closer. "With you."

Hekla's stomach whirled and looped, but she forced her mind to the lesson she'd learned long ago—a pretty face was *not* to be trusted.

Reaching for the bravado she'd sculpted over the years, Hekla arched a brow. "You looking for a fight or a roll in the furs, warrior?"

"Why not both?" He smirked and dipped beneath the water's surface, leaving Hekla to stare at the rippling waters.

Heat pooled between her thighs, and she hated how much

she wanted this man. And she could not help but recall the last time she'd brought Gunnar to her bed. His kisses had been eager, but as Hekla undressed, he broke down in tears. Suffice it to say, her lust was instantly extinguished. Instead of crying out in pleasure, she'd held him as he cried on her shoulder.

For weeks, Hekla had been trying to hold the pieces of the Bloodaxe Crew together in the aftermath of Ilías's death, and gods, it had been exhausting. Why shouldn't she take something for herself? Live for herself tonight? Perhaps a few mind-bending orgasms would put her back to rights.

The man emerged from the water, startlingly close. "Well?" he asked, scraping his hair back and watching her expectantly. Water droplets caught in his unfairly thick lashes and cut paths down his sculpted chest.

Hekla stepped nearer. She reached for the hem of his tunic, but the man's hand wrapped around her left wrist. He yanked her forward and her chest collided with the solid expanse of his. Her body tingled with anticipation as a large hand slid up her spine and came to rest on her nape. Slowly, almost cautiously, the warrior leaned down. His lips brushed against hers, and heat danced through her.

His fingers tightened on her neck, a low sound breaking in the back of his throat. Whatever he felt, she felt it, too. Like every quiet corner of her body had suddenly awakened. Colors bloomed on the backs of her eyelids as his fingers slid into her hair, and he tilted her jaw so he could deepen the kiss. As his tongue delved into her mouth, Hekla matched his movements with her own.

Lust settled low and heavy inside her, and Hekla reached again for his tunic. This time, the warrior didn't stop her. She peeled it over his head, revealing an expanse of olive skin and a ruthlessly toned body. She ran her fingers appreciatively over his skin and braced as his mouth crashed down on hers.

The man kissed with unexpected passion, like he was facing death, and she was his last meal. And gods, but Hekla longed to be consumed. Time grew slippery as she lost herself in the warrior's kiss and the feel of his hands exploring her body. Eventually, the man drew back with a question in his eyes.

"More," she whispered, tugging him to her.

The warrior's fingers slid down her spine and reached for the hem of her tunic. He shucked it off with startling speed, and it landed on the riverbank with a loud slap.

"I don't even know your name," muttered the man, mouth sliding down the column of her throat.

"Nor I yours," she breathed, tilting her head back. "Let us keep it that way. No names; only us."

He pulled back, hazel eyes searching her face. The warrior looked uncertain, as though he meant to say something, but as Hekla's hand delved into his breeches, only a groan escaped him.

"Or," she whispered, her hand encircling his hardened shaft, "I will call you Fox, and you can call me Lynx."

"Fox?" The man groaned as her hand moved.

"Your sparring proves you've a cunning streak." Hekla watched the man's beautiful face contort as she began to stroke him in earnest.

"And Lynx?" asked the man through heavy-lidded eyes.

Hekla chuckled softly. "Armed with deadly sharp parts."

"The lynx is predator to the fox."

"Mmm. Best not to turn your back on me."

"You're astonishing." The man chuckled, but his gaze grew weighted. He reached for her breeches, pausing at the clasp.

"Magnetic," breathed Hekla.

"Clever." The Fox flicked the clasp open. One hand slid down, and then it was Hekla's turn to moan as the warrior stroked her softly.

The water was cool, yet her body steamed beneath the Fox's touch. Already it seemed he could read her every response, and she had the inkling that they were locked in a new sort of challenge: Who would drive the other to pleasure first?

As the heel of the Fox's palm rubbed against her most sensitive part, Hekla was helpless against the moan rising in her throat. Her thumb rubbed along the tip of his cock, satisfaction welling as his whole body shuddered. Their faces were bare inches apart, breaths mingling together. He looked at her with such directness, the weight of his gaze so intimate. It should make Hekla squirm, but instead it made heat unfurl within her.

The Fox found that sensitive spot deep inside her, and Hekla gasped as pleasure began to spool tightly.

She pumped harder, stroking him faster. She just needed another minute. Another full-body tremble rolled through the Fox, but Hekla's glee was short-lived.

"Come for me, Lynx," he whispered.

And Hekla fell apart.

Her insides contracted; all thoughts obliterated as warm, pulsing heat rushed through her body. Her eyes fell shut as her senses unraveled with ecstasy. She could *feel* colors—bright pulsing rings of violet that suffused through her veins, the taste of sweet strawberries bursting on her tongue.

For those mindless moments after she found pleasure, everything was hazy. Hekla was that young woman once more—the one who read romantic tales of knights and princesses and true love. Her head was filled with dreams, her heart open to love. She was soft and vulnerable and so completely open.

But slowly, Hekla's vision swam back into focus to find eyes filled with delight and discovery.

"You're rather sensitive, aren't you, Lynx?" whispered the Fox, fingers moving higher to stroke the smooth skin of her stomach.

"Am I?" Dazed, Hekla remained in his arms, relenting to his gentle touch.

"Aye. And it makes me wonder"—the green in his hazel eyes seemed to brighten—"how many times can I make you moan like that?" His hand moved from her stomach to smooth a wet tendril of hair from her brow.

Hekla tensed, the tenderness pulling her firmly back in the moment. But she concealed her reaction with a mischievous smile. "You win this round, Foxie," she said, eyes gleaming as her hand moved back to his shaft. "But I assure you, you shall not win the next."

"Is that a challenge, Lynx?" It sounded as though he had gravel in his throat.

Good. She bit down on her smile. "It's a promise, Fox."

And as an agonized look crossed the man's beautiful face—as he bucked into her hold with a low, guttural moan—Hekla knew they weren't nearly done sparring.

CHAPTER SIX

Present Day

The yard behind the Hungry Blade was bright with the rising sun, the light catching golden leaves on the old tree beyond the fence. It was early for the leaves to turn—easy to forget it hadn't been long since the Bloodaxe Crew had celebrated the Longest Day. Hekla's chest clenched tight at that thought, and she forced her attention to the yard.

The clash of steel vibrated the air. Hakonsson's men had paired off and were sparring, but to Hekla's dismay, she failed to find Sigrún and Gunnar among them. With a long exhale, she tried to quell her disappointment. Gunnar had seemed more upbeat this morning; Sigrún a pillar of stoic resilience. For a small moment, Hekla had felt the Bloodaxe Crew back at her side, and gods, but it had been such a relief.

She straightened her spine and strolled among the warriors. They had good form, their movements crisp and laced with power. It was clear they were well trained. But as one warrior's armor caught the sunlight, Hekla shielded her eyes.

"Better put that armor to use, warrior," she said dryly. "Get some scuff marks on it before you blind someone with it."

The man and his opponent paused, two pairs of steely eyes slicing into her skin. She recognized one as the warrior who'd shared her bench at the daymeal. He frowned, assessing her.

"I suppose you'd like to try, *woman*?"

Hekla let out a heavy sigh. As a woman in a mercenary crew, it often went this way. And perhaps it was her good fortune she'd inadvertently insulted the largest warrior in Eyvind's retinue. Because Hekla knew she'd have to make an example of him.

The yard had quieted, and Hekla felt the whole of the retinue watching her. Good. She'd show them how a woman fought. All that *emotion* had to be channeled somewhere.

Hekla put a hand on her waist, popping her hip. "I'm Hekla," she told the man, batting her eyelashes. "And your name, blue eyes?"

His eyes narrowed in clear suspicion. "Thrand Long Sword. Eyvind's second."

"Long Sword?" Hekla smirked, glancing at his groin. "Trying to compensate for something, are you?"

A chorus of incredulous laughter filled the air. The warm undertones of Thrand's tawny complexion seemed to flush darker. He concealed his humiliation with a twirl of his sword.

"I'd challenge you to combat, but I don't fight women."

He turned his back on her, a gesture of such disrespect it made Hekla's blood simmer with rage. But she forced calm into her voice as she called out, "Or perhaps you're simply afraid you'll lose."

She'd uttered these words more times than she cared to

count, and so Hekla was unsurprised when they had the desired effect. Slowly, Thrand turned, his blue eyes hard as shards of ice. The whole of the yard watched the pair of them. There was no way Thrand could back away from this challenge now.

"Come and say that to my face," he gritted out.

Hekla strolled toward the man, swaying her hips. Thrand widened his stance, his sword grip tightening. She skimmed her metal fingers beneath the warrior's jaw. A subtle click of the button on the underside of her prosthetic's wrist, and her claws shot out, grazing the tender skin of his throat. Though Thrand's jaw tightened, the warrior held his ground in a way she respected.

"I challenge you to combat, Thrand *Long Sword*."

And with that, Hekla retracted her claws and sauntered back a few steps.

Thrand didn't take his gaze off her as the nearby warriors retreated, creating a space around him and Hekla. She shook out her body, her blood flowing with vigor. Perhaps what she'd truly needed all these days was a taste of shattered male ego. It was so delicious, after all.

"I accept," said Thrand with a scowl. He glanced at his sparring partner uncertainly. But as his gaze landed back on Hekla, it hardened. "No shields. No blades. No *claws*." He nodded at her prosthetic hand.

"Aw," said Hekla, with mock disappointment. "Don't tell me you're afraid of a little scratch, Long Sword." She sighed. "Very well. I shall keep them sheathed."

A nearly imperceptible nod from the man, and then, "First blood wins."

They squared off, staring at each other with equal intensity. Hekla's muscles filled with energy as she sank into her battle mindset—a place where instinct and intelligence entwined. She watched Thrand's every blink, noted the way his enormous hands splayed restlessly at his sides.

A whistle pierced the air. And then it was mayhem.

Thrand lunged at her with speed and strength, but Hekla saw it coming from a mile away. Sliding under his grip, she shoved her shoulder into his gut before spinning away. But the lout was quick to recover, whirling on her in time to dodge her striking fist.

Hekla lost herself to this dance, the careful balance of aggression and protection. She knew well enough how it felt to be on the receiving end of a blow from a man his size. Minutes ticked by, the pair circling each other as sweat dripped from their brows, and the crowd watched eagerly.

Hekla knew she'd find no support among them, but that was all right. She was used to being the underdog. In fact, she thrived on it. What she couldn't stomach was the way Thrand held himself back. Was he truly so afraid of harming a woman?

"Is that all you've got, Long Sword?" taunted Hekla, wagging her little finger at him.

Thrand took the bait, throwing himself at her with a growl.

But there was something about the pitch of the growl, paired with the sweet scent of decomposing leaves, that triggered a memory long buried in Hekla.

For a heartbeat, she was sent back in time. Golden light streaming through autumn leaves. Woodsmoke and the smell of róa drifting through the windows and into the yard. Hekla had fresh eggs bundled in her apron dress as she made her way across the yard. The first light of day was near blinding, and yet Rothna had not yet returned from the mead hall.

Her husband's low growl was her only warning before Hekla was shoved from behind. She tripped and went sprawling, eggs spattering beneath her. Hekla rolled and stared up at her husband. And there loomed Rothna in all his glory, his scowl telling her just how many sólas he'd lost at the tables. He'd be looking for a scapegoat, so Hekla was unsurprised when her husband drew back his fist.

Stars burst in her vision, but it was *Thrand's* fist that swung through the blow. Thrand who now ambled toward her, a conflicted look in his eyes. As Hekla blinked, trying to shake off the intrusive memory, Thrand's burly arm wrapped around her neck and yanked her against his chest.

"I do this as a favor to you," he growled in her ear. "You must learn that women have no place in a warband."

His words yanked Hekla back into her body, anger and fire raging through her blood.

"Yield," he demanded.

With a scream, she drove her fist into Thrand's groin, just as she'd trained Silla to do all those times on the Road of Bones. The warrior let out a high-pitched wail.

"Pitiful male weakness," she grunted against his grip.

Despite his agony, Thrand had enough presence of mind to keep his arm wrapped around her neck.

"There's something you ought to have asked me, Thrand," said Hekla, loud enough for all to hear. "My full name. My Bloodaxe name."

She gathered all her energy. Yanked Thrand forward. Then used all her momentum to ram her elbow into his ribs. The soft crack told her it had landed true. The warrior howled, and Hekla wrenched free.

She whirled on Thrand, now bent double and clutching his side.

"They call me Rib Smasher."

CHAPTER SEVEN

Wind whipped across Hekla's cheeks, the rhythmic clop of hooves in her ears as her mount followed a much-subdued Thrand along the road. The man was utterly dramatic, hunched in the saddle and rubbing his side every five minutes. Hekla huffed a breath. It wasn't as though he'd suffered a death blow. Although, as she considered it, perhaps it *had* been a death blow to his precious ego.

Eyvind had heard a commotion in the yard, exiting the mead hall just in time to witness Hekla putting Thrand in his place. To her surprise, Eyvind had thrown his head back and laughed, before proclaiming he would buy the finest ale the Hungry Blade had to offer for whoever had just bested his second in command.

As his gaze settled on Hekla, Eyvind quieted, that look of surprise and discovery mingling in his expression. But Konal was suddenly there as well, bellowing his displeasure and reminding Eyvind to get control of his warriors.

Hekla hadn't stayed long enough to hear Eyvind's reply. She'd accomplished what she'd set out to do this morning. After her display in the yard, Eyvind's retinue knew she was not to be trifled with.

Now they were en route to the Braksson steading, the site of the mist's second attack. Sigrún rode silently on Hekla's left, the hood of her cloak drawn up despite the warmth of the sunshine.

What do you think of the new leader? signed Sigrún, glancing Eyvind's way.

I think he's a pompous arse, Hekla signed back. *And I do not think his warriors are tried in battle.*

Sigrún sighed wearily. For a moment, Hekla was desperate to know what was going on in her Bloodaxe sister's mind. She could not forget Sigrún's face—ghostly white—in the moments following Ilías's death. She'd fled into the woods and had not returned until first light. And though she was here in body, it was clear Sigrún had not been here in mind since that horrible day.

Are you—Hekla paused, searching for the right word to sign—*comfortable around these new warriors?* It was clunky and too forward for fiercely private Sigrún, but Hekla did not know how to ask any other way.

I'm fine, signed Sigrún briskly.

Rebuked, Hekla forced her gaze straight ahead. She ought to have expected as much. Even after five years of fighting together, she still knew so little about Sigrún. But as the petite blond warrior sighed once again, Hekla turned back toward her.

I hate this, signed Sigrún. *Axe Eyes should be here. No Beard. The Wolf. It is not the same without them.*

An ache built in Hekla's chest, and she tried to rub it away.

I do not like strangers, continued Sigrún, and Hekla had the vague realization that this was more than the woman had ever shared with her. *How can I trust these men when I cannot even communicate with them?*

A breath hissed between Hekla's teeth, and she felt like a fool. *I am sorry,* Hekla signed. *I will do better at staying nearby to interpret for them.*

Sigrún waved her hand in casual dismissal. *I do not need you to fight my battles,* she signed, then paused. *Though I thank you for the offer.*

Now it was Hekla's turn to sigh. She stared at the empty space to her right—the space where Gunnar should be riding.

Gunnar will be all right, signed Sigrún, following her gaze. *He only needs time.*

I told Hakonsson that Gunnar was ill, Hekla signed, her insides twisting. *But I do not know how long he'll accept such excuses.* She chewed her lip, pondering how she could help him—what she could do or say to help Gunnar find his way back to himself.

As the Brakssons' steading came into view, Hekla ground her teeth together. She'd visited this farm countless times—had examined each timber beam in the longhouse and each blade of straw in the bloody barn. Today would be an exercise in futility.

"I will be patient," she muttered to herself. "I will fall in line."

Beside her, a chuffing sound came from Sigrún—one Hekla knew as her Bloodaxe sister's laugh. "Quiet, you," she grumbled. "I can do it."

The sun shone pleasantly down from cloud-flecked skies across the farm. Everything was precisely as it had been the last time they'd visited: a vacant pen that had once housed sheep; an overturned cart that would have been used to haul barley, had the Brakssons lived to see the harvest.

Each time Hekla set foot on one of Istré's farmsteads, nostalgia swirled within her like crisp autumn leaves. If she squinted just right, she could see her father and brother, toiling in the fields, her grandmother hanging washing on the line. That was the *before*—before the sickness had stolen her father and grandmother. Before her brother had married Hekla off to Rothna. Back then, she'd been a girl filled with dreams. Now she was a woman who'd seen too much.

Hekla dismounted and shielded her eyes as she surveyed the Braksson fields bordering the Western Woods. It was barley and, like all other crops in Íseldur these days, severely stunted. With a sigh, Hekla led her mare to where Eyvind and his retinue had secured their horses.

The quiet blanketing the farmstead made her skin prickle. No birds chirped from the surrounding trees; no insects buzzed in the grass. It had the feeling of . . . *nothing*. After securing her horse, Hekla trailed Eyvind's men into the longhouse. Konal leaned against a wall, arms folded over his chest as he glowered in her direction.

Look your fill, graybeard, she told him with her eyes. And when the man looked away first, Hekla's lips tilted up in victory. But her smile fell as her gaze landed on Loftur standing near the hearth with a hand raised for silence. Conversation died, and Istré's chieftain launched into the same drivel Hekla had endured for weeks already. She could not sit in this barren home listening to another moment of it.

"Heading to the privy," Hekla lied to Thrand. "The daymeal does not sit well."

Hekla tried not to roll her eyes at Thrand's appalled expression. Such prim city warriors. With a sigh, she stalked out of the longhouse.

"Blood spatter everywhere," Loftur was saying, his voice drifting through the windows. "As you can see, the claw marks groove too deeply to be of human origin."

Hekla had just reached the privy when movement amid the stillness of the woods caught her eye. Under ordinary conditions, she would think nothing of it. A forest, after all, should be teeming with life. But not *this* forest. The hairs on her arms stood on end.

"I will be patient," she reminded herself, continuing her path toward the privy. But Hekla could not resist another glance toward the woods. There it was again—a small creature hopping in the underbrush. After weeks without any sign of life in or around these woods, curiosity bristled through her.

Hekla threw a cautious look over her shoulder, then moved swiftly toward the trees. She would not enter the forest. She would only peer through the trees to identify the creature.

As she neared, her pulse quickened. Her eyes strained as she searched for the source of movement. But after a long minute spent gazing into the shadows, Hekla decided it must have been a trick of her mind. With a sigh, she began to turn.

Then she saw it.

Carved into the crusted trunk of a pine not two paces into the woods was a symbol. With a spiral center and eight branching arms, there was no question of what it was.

"A Spiral Stave," Hekla murmured, staring hard. It was the

same symbol that had been scrawled in blood on the Klaernar's corpses in Istré's town square. A sigil that had once belonged to the Volsik bloodline.

Running a hand along her braid, Hekla glanced over her shoulder. The warriors were still in the longhouse, Loftur still droning on. Her gaze fell yet again to the forest. The knowing feeling rose from deep inside her—the same feeling that told her Loftur was hiding something. The Spiral Stave was a clue to be followed. Yet if she played by Eyvind's rules, she'd be forced to wait.

Irritation churned in her stomach. Hekla cursed herself for promising Eyvind she'd fall in line. Who would pay the price for a lengthy investigation? Innocent Istré citizens, like Halldora and Onund Ale Drinker. All while Loftur the Bloody "Bird-Witted" sat in his high seat and drank ale.

Her decision was made. Hekla drew a deep breath and stepped into the woods.

So much for playing by the rules.

CHAPTER EIGHT

Two steps into the Western Woods, Hekla pulled her cloak tighter around her shoulders. The legends her grandmother had once told her rang loudly in her ears—frightening and fascinating tales of mythical creatures, of sacred groves and deep-rooted magic.

"They are only stories," Hekla murmured to herself, though her hand found the hilt of her sword all the same.

Towering pines swayed above bare-branched rowans, vibrant red berries the lone spot of color in these eerie woods. Sunlight slanted high through the trees, catching on lichen-covered branches. But the forest floor told a different story. Bone-dry moss and dead leaves crunched beneath Hekla's feet while the corpse limbs of bracken ferns rasped eerily against tree trunks. Ferns and shrubs, tree saplings and mushrooms—all of them were dead. The forest floor was a graveyard.

Hekla peered at the sun-dappled pine boughs above. Whatever plagued the smaller plants clearly had not yet claimed the larger, hardier trees. After one last glance back at the farmstead, she forced herself onward, weaving between the stems and tracking deeper into the woods. It did not take long for her to find the second Spiral Stave carved into a trunk. Her body tingled with excitement, the knowing feeling inside her only growing more certain: The path she walked led to answers.

As she strode on, Hekla searched the darkness for any sign of the creature she'd spied at the edge of the woods, her hand never lifting from the hilt of her sword. She listened for the telltale sound of the mist—that eerie muffled heartbeat—yet it was as though a blanket of silence had fallen upon the forest. No birds. No small woodland creatures. Her gaze landed on a third Spiral Stave, and she pressed onward.

The air grew thicker, tinged with a heavy, earthen scent. In the depths of the woods, the pine trees dominated, their toothy needles clawing toward the sun. By the time Hekla spotted the sixth Spiral Stave, the forest was altogether gloomy.

Then she heard the scrape of dead brush—brittle twigs snapping like bones. Hekla unsheathed her sword, widened her stance, and held herself absolutely still. As she stared into the thick brambles, she wondered if her mind was playing tricks on her. Then a whiskered nose peeked out from beneath a twitching bush.

"A squirrel."

Hekla chuffed in disbelief. Burning fucking stars. She'd drawn her sword on a bloody squirrel.

With a heavy exhale, she soldiered forward, eyes searching for the next Spiral Stave. By now Eyvind would have discovered her absence, and Loftur would be fuming. Hekla's stomach twinged with a hint of regret, but she'd come too far to turn back now. Besides, for the first time in weeks, she was *doing* something.

The next Spiral Stave was carved into the trunk of an ancient pine. Dry leaves scraped along the forest floor, and she whirled around. The squirrel was a few paces behind her, its russet tail twitching.

"Get out of here!" Hekla waved her arms to frighten it off, but the squirrel stood its ground, watching her with beady black eyes. With an irritated sigh, Hekla turned back to her task. The underbrush grew denser, sharp brambles grasping at her cloak and breeches. Finally, Hekla broke through into a clearing.

Instantly, the air lightened, the scent shifting from acrid pine needles to sweet summer blossoms. Hekla blinked at the soft emerald moss carpeting the clearing. Why was it not dead and brittle like in the forest beyond? Indeed, compared to the gnarled gloom of the outer forest, this clearing had the sense of a refuge—an island of calm in wild seas.

In the center of the clearing stood an enormous tree. Not a pine, nor a rowan; Hekla had never seen anything like it. The tree's thick trunk twisted upward, a handful of yellowing leaves clinging to long, curving branches. Her eyes traced along the tree's bark, and a jolt ran through her. Another Spiral Stave. It wasn't carved like the others. This one was twisted into the gnarled whorls of the trunk itself.

Hekla's mind swirled with unanswerable questions. Who had killed the Klaernar and scrawled the Spiral Staves in their blood? Had their aim been to draw someone to this clearing all along? Despite the lack of answers, her skin buzzed with anticipation as she lifted her hand and grazed her fingers along the rough bark.

Energy surged into her body, her mind flooding with a

thousand memories that were not her own: groves of elder trees so enormous their branches scraped the clouds and their roots burrowed to the deepest depths of the earth; a forest teeming with life, with birds and skarplings; frost foxes and flíta; glossy beetles marching over delicate mushroom caps and white lichen unfurling under moonlight. In the forest's rich soil, insects wriggled—life-forms too small to see with the living eye thrived. Delicate threads connected each plant in the forest, nourishment pulsing through them from elder to sapling. She was slumbering on a bed of moss and lichen, her grimwolves all around her, thick gray coats rising and falling with each rhythmic breath.

But beneath it all, a low, shrill sound built with each beat of her heart. Horror and anger and desperation thrashed through her. The cycle reversed—nourishment stolen, sucked from the forest, an unending hunger, devouring all in its path. It was coming for her, too, eager to Turn her to its cause. She had to protect herself at all costs, even if it meant going dormant to survive. The sound reached its apex, a bloodcurdling screech that was the sound of nightmares. And at last Hekla understood—the scream was coming from the tree.

She stumbled back with a gasp. The woods swarmed back into view, and Hekla clutched her hand to her chest, staring at the tree. Had she lost her gods-damned mind? But the feel of coarse wolf hair lingered on her fingertips, the despair and rage still churning through her blood.

The squirrel chittered from a branch on the strange tree, and Hekla leaped back. Red tail twitching in agitation, it released another string of angry sounds.

It was time to leave. Hekla turned on her heel just as the ground beneath her rumbled. She was filled with prickling awareness, swiftly followed by the sense of being hunted.

A low, steady thump sounded distantly from within the woods.

No, thought Hekla, desperation clawing through her. It couldn't be. But the pulsing grew louder, and Hekla knew she was not imagining it.

The mist was coming.

Her hand moved to the hilt of her sword, yet she knew there was no weapon to vanquish this foe. None had survived the mist's deadly embrace. Her only chance was to flee.

Hekla drew her sword anyway and hacked at the brambles encircling the clearing, desperate to get back into the open forest so she could run. The heartbeat's rhythm picked up, though the beat was still distant. But the sound of it climbed up through her boots and vibrated her bones.

I'm coming for you, it seemed to say.

Ripping her cloak free from a sharp branch, Hekla burst out of the thicket, stumbling between branches and over rocks. But she was in the open forest, and an ember of hope sparked to life. The battle thrill coursed through her veins, powering her limbs. She had to get out of these woods. Had to get away from the mist. Had to warn the others so they could get to safety. She passed a familiar stump, recognized a distinct, forked rowan, but Hekla knew she was still too far from the Brakssons' steading, that the pulsating beat grew too rapid . . .

She cast a desperate look over her shoulder and immediately wished she hadn't. Thick white mist slithered between tree trunks with impossible speed. And in that moment, she knew: Escaping this thing was not possible.

Hekla had never been one to run from death. And so, she paused. Turned to face it.

"Well met," she said, hefting her sword.

The mist undulated in time with the rapid heartbeat, sweeping closer. But Hekla held her ground. Greeted her destiny. Swung her blade as the mist engulfed her.

It was much like being plunged underwater, only in reverse. She emerged from the deathly stillness of the woods into utter chaos. Discordant sounds assaulted her ears, while monstrous creatures danced around her. Inside the mist, the forest transformed into a place of devastation. Trees, bald and lifeless; moss, gray and crisped. Beneath it all, a webwork of black fire was woven in the soil.

The pulsating rhythm of the mist was distant yet all around her, its anger growing faster with the beat. She could feel it permeating her senses, invading her throat, and seeping into her skin. It searched out the tethers of her life force and free will, eager to break and reforge—to Turn her to its cause. Nausea overwhelming her, Hekla sank to her knees, all hope bleeding from her slowly. Nothing could save her from the mist.

She was filled with too many emotions to count: dismay that rather than protect Istré's people, she'd only join the ranks of their dead; a strange sense of emptiness she did not care to examine too closely; but most potent of all was her gladness that she would leave this realm with a sword in her hand. She'd chosen this life, and thus, this death. And with that, a curious sense of peace drowned out the chaos.

But as Hekla readied herself for death, a snarl met her ears, air brushing her face as a large figure leaped past her. Hekla blinked. It was an enormous grimwolf, its size rivaling a horse's. In sharp contrast to the dying forest all around her, this wolf teemed with vitality. With light.

The mist hissed with anger, repelled from the beast's form. The wolf turned. Met Hekla's gaze with bright yellow eyes.

Cover your ears. Close your eyes, said a voice in her head.

Dazed, Hekla obeyed.

A thunderous sound filled the air all around her as a lightning-bright shock rippled down her spine. And then, she knew no more.

CHAPTER NINE

When Hekla's eyes fluttered open, she was certain she was dead. Yet if this was death, why did she feel like she'd been trampled by wild horses?

She blinked to clear her vision, searching for the stars. Wasn't that what people believed? That she'd follow the Mother Star and settle among her ancestors? But as an evergreen canopy came into view, as her lungs filled with loamy air, an alarming thought filled her mind. Was she in the Bear God's Sacred Forest? Gods, she hoped not.

Hekla propped herself up on her elbows, vision warping. She blinked. The squirrel lay motionless beside her.

"Oh!" She bolted up and brushed a knuckle along the creature's side. The rodent's chest expanded with a breath, and relief filled her. A few more strokes of her knuckles, and the squirrel's eyes fluttered open. Hekla found her waterskin and poured a small amount into the lid. Holding the cap carefully next to the squirrel, she waited. The creature blinked at the water, then dipped its nose into the cap, those beady black eyes looking at Hekla as it drank.

Slowly, Hekla's bearings came back to her. Brittle moss beneath her, evergreens swaying above her. She was cold beyond measure and utterly exhausted. But the mist was gone, and she was alive. It felt like a dream, and yet she was left with more questions than when she'd entered this gods-damned forest.

The squirrel sat upright, and Hekla realized it had drained all the water in the cap. She refilled it and watched as the squirrel drank more. After a while it sat back on its haunches, a bristly red tail twitching behind it.

Protector is very kind to Kritka, came a childlike voice inside her mind. *Kritka banished the dark thing, but it took much strength.*

Hekla stared at the squirrel, the chill in her bones seeming to grow with each punishing throb at her temples. Surely, she was dreaming. Struck with a sudden wave of dizziness, Hekla lay back down, resting her cheek on brittle moss. Gods, but she was cold and so very tired.

The squirrel bounded into her line of vision.

The dark thing will send its creatures, said the voice. *Protector must leave. Come back another day.*

Hekla wanted to laugh at this strange phantom vision, but she was too tired. She needed to close her eyes. Rest for a moment . . .

"Hekla!"

Her eyes flew open in time to see the squirrel's russet tail vanishing beneath a dead shrub. The chill had truly sunk its claws into her now. She curled into a ball. Teeth chattering, Hekla wondered if she'd ever been so cold in her life. What was it Silla did? Think hearthfire thoughts?

Hekla tried to imagine a hearthfire. Tried to remember what it felt like to be warm. But she was wrung out, as though she'd just fought the most arduous battle of her life. And perhaps she had. Surely, she deserved to sleep, just for a little while.

"Hekla!"

The voice cut through the silence like a greataxe, its echo pulsing in her skull. The trees swayed back and forth, and a chill prickled through her. When the voice called again, Hekla rallied all the strength she could.

"Here!" she called out. "I'm here!"

A twig snapped, footsteps crunching on moss, then a figure with hazel eyes loomed over her.

"Foxie," she croaked.

Eyvind crouched before her, a thunderous expression upon his stupidly beautiful face. "Mulish woman." His expression shifted to concern. "Where are you hurt?" Those large hands ran along her body, searching for injuries.

Hekla stared up at him. "Your eyes are like gemstones," she mumbled.

"Gods, you're burning up." The back of his hand pressed to her forehead, and she nuzzled against it.

"You feel like a hearthfire." A violent shiver racked her body, and it felt as though she'd never been warm in her life . . . like she'd never be again. But this man had heated her through. Had made her trust, if only for a night . . .

"This fever . . . I must get you to a healer."

The trees swayed as he hefted her into his arms, cradling her against his chest like she was a gods-damned damsel in distress. His smell surrounded her, the planes of his chest solid against her cheek. Too close. Too much. She couldn't . . . she wouldn't . . .

"No." She pushed against his chest, but his hold was ironclad. "Let me walk."

"You cannot even stand. Determined to be a pain in my arse, aren't you, Lynx?"

Trees flew by, the foliage jostling above them. The man was running through the forest with a grown woman in his arms. Distantly, Hekla recognized this was an impressive feat. But the thought flitted away with the rest of them, and she was pressing her cheek into his tunic, sinking lower, lower.

"Stay with me, Lynx," he panted as the minutes bled together. "Tell me what happened."

"Spiral Stave," she mumbled. "You must follow them—"

"The mist," he said sharply. "We heard the heartbeat. Tell me it didn't touch you."

Thick white mist filled her mind's eye, that insatiable hunger impossible to forget. A moan slid from her lips, and she curled toward him. Toward safety.

No. Not safety. She made her *own* safety. Hekla shuddered, then tried again to escape his grasp.

"Stop squirming, woman. Tell me about the mist."

"Wolf," she managed. *Squirrel,* she thought, but did not have the strength to say it aloud. That voice rang in her ears once more. *Kritka banished the dark thing, but it took much strength.*

"Stay with me, Hekla."

But the cold was absolute, a blanket of darkness settling all around her.

"Fight, Hekla. Do not give in."

It wasn't giving in when it was inevitable. When it was destiny—when it was warmth, and she was so very cold.

"Gods damn it, Lynx!"

And then, she was gone.

The skies were black and moonless, and the air held a smothering feel. The darkness was more than a mere absence of light—it was a living thing, its heartbeat throbbing in time with her own. Or perhaps it was merely the drumbeat filling the air as Hekla walked through Istré's streets.

She wove between revelers toward the town square. V-shaped pillars loomed before her, and she passed grappling warriors, playing their fighting games. The drums seemed to drive her movements. Forward, she stepped. Onward, she moved. Until she stood before it. The dais.

A grand oak table had been set on the dais, feast fare spread upon it. Loftur ruled from his high seat, Eyvind and Konal flanking him. The pulsing beat was like a hook in her belly, pulling Hekla up the stairs and into a chair beside Eyvind.

"A toast," bellowed Loftur, lifting his cup, "to the old gods!"

The crowd shouted their approval, and as Hekla drank her wine, her ears caught something above the din. A heartbeat.

Hekla opened her mouth to warn them, but it was too late. Thick white mist slithered all around them, its hunger filling the air. It darted forward. Slid down Eyvind's throat. Hazel eyes bulged. She could hear the tear of muscle and sinew, the crack of bones. Eyvind had to be broken before he could be remade.

"Forsaken!" screamed Loftur, climbing over the table. "The old gods have forsaken us!"

But Hekla could not take her eyes from Eyvind. He thrashed and bellowed, clawed at his own skin. Eyvind drew a tremendous, shuddering breath. Then stilled.

And when he turned to her, his eyes glowed like the red embers of a fire.

Wake, said a childlike voice.

Hekla awoke with a gasp. Her heart pounded as though it tried to hack free from her chest, horror and panic churning violently through her blood. But rather than the dark, forbidding canopy of a half-dead forest, her eyes met a sliver of daylight on timber beams. She followed the light to the covered window, then to the small, furry rodent perched on the ledge before it. The creature's tail twitched.

"You're awake!"

Hekla's gaze swung to Gunnar—whose face was etched with pure relief—then back to the window.

The ledge was empty.

Hekla rubbed her eyes and took in her surroundings. Aged timber beams above her. Wolfskin furs draped over her. The faint smell of woodsmoke and cooked food in the air. She was back in her chambers at the inn, with Gunnar and Sigrún hovering over her bed.

"What happened?" Hekla winced at the throb in her temples as she tried to sit up.

We might ask you the same, signed Sigrún. *When Hakonsson carried you from the woods, you were unconscious and burning with fever.*

That explained her aching muscles and pulsating skull.

He brought you back to Istré on his horse. Put you to bed. Fetched a healer, then kicked the healer out.

"He . . . what?"

Sigrún glanced at Gunnar before signing, *After a full day and night, the local healer said there was nothing he could do for you. Hakonsson was angered and sent his second to fetch a new one.*

Hekla's insides rolled. "And the new healer?"

Steeped a mushroom tea and used a cloth to drip it into your mouth. Sigrún's brown eyes held uncharacteristic emotion. *It was a long night, but your fever broke in the morning.* She paused. *I think they saved your life.*

Hekla let out a shaky exhale, pressing her fingers to her temples. Saved her life.

"Hek—" Gunnar's voice cracked. "I'm . . . we're . . . we cannot lose you, too!"

He leaped forward and pulled her into a forceful hug. Hekla blinked back her shock as Gunnar buried his face in her neck, incoherent words coming between his sobs. Hesitantly, Hekla patted his locs, meeting Sigrún's amused gaze over his shoulder.

Gunnar and I have been talking. Sigrún's jaw hardened before her hands signed with swift, confident gestures, *We've let everything fall on your shoulders. We haven't been there for you. We will do better, Hekla, we promise it.*

Her words meant more than Hekla could say. The past few weeks had been so isolating. Perhaps it had made Hekla more impatient . . . more reckless than she ought to have been.

Hekla nodded, trying to extract herself from Gunnar's clutches. But the warrior did not seem inclined to let her go. "Let me breathe, you oaf."

Reluctantly, Gunnar released her and batted a tear from his cheek. "I thought you were going to die!"

"I've survived far worse. It'll take more than a fever to bring me down, Fire Fist."

"Aye, but it will." Gunnar looked at her fondly, a certain glimmer back in his eye. Gods, but she was glad to see it. Glad to have them both in this room.

"Gather yourself, Gunnar," Hekla teased. "What would No Beard say?" The words slipped out carelessly, and Hekla wished she could claw them back.

A silence filled the room, so heavy it felt like a tangible thing. Hekla's throat closed up, and in that moment, she missed Ilías as fiercely as the day they'd buried him. She closed her eyes, hating herself as she had a thousand times before. Too loud, too forward, *too much,* as always, and now she'd trampled Gunnar's fragile sense of peace.

Hekla waited for the large warrior to fall to pieces—readied herself to be strong for him—but Gunnar surprised her.

"I reckon," he said, "Ilías'd tell me I'm uglier than my mother when I cry."

There was a moment of silence, like the peace following a wave's crash ashore. Then Hekla tossed her head back and laughed. Gunnar and Sigrún soon joined in. It was a strange, purifying laugh—one that felt like the first step toward a new normal. It wouldn't be easy. Wouldn't be the same as before. But this collective laugh promised it would be *something*.

Wiping tears from her eyes, Hekla shook her head. "That's exactly what he'd say."

"We're here now, Hek," said Gunnar, his voice growing serious. "We're in it with you."

Hekla looked from Gunnar wiping snot on his sleeve, to Sigrún dabbing discreetly at the corner of her eye. "The next time I get grand plans in my head," she said, "I'll come to you two first."

Good, signed Sigrún. *You need warriors you can trust at your back.*

"Aye, but I do," muttered Hekla. She drew a deep breath.

And then she told them everything.

CHAPTER TEN

Hekla's nose wrinkled as she sipped the bitter mushroom tea. The healer—the second one, that was—had left a small satchel of withered brown stems along with directions to take a daily cup of the stuff for a full week after her fever had broken. And while a daily cup of tea was well and good, his instructions for a week of bedrest were quickly discarded.

She'd bathed and eaten a hearty bowl of stew. And after a glorious afternoon nap, she now tried to gather her energy. Leaning against her headboard, Hekla found herself staring at the window, searching for any trace of the phantom squirrel. She nearly laughed at the thought. Obviously, it had been a fever-induced vision.

Now that the sun had set, sounds of laughter and revelry filtered into her room. Hekla had spent three days and nights in slumber, which made this the fifth consecutive night of the Winter Nights celebrations. They were only two nights away from the penultimate feast.

"I gather Loftur has continued his quest to drain Istré of all its winter provisions," she muttered to Sigrún, forcing another sip of the strange tea.

They've been brawling and feasting each night, if that's what you're asking, signed Sigrún with a scowl.

"Gods above. How can that man truly think the old gods will swoop in and save them?"

It seems like Hakonsson is in Loftur's pocket, signed Sigrún.

Hekla frowned. "I cannot understand how Axe Eyes thought him suitable to lead this investigation. It's maddening!"

Sigrún and Gunnar nodded their agreement, then relayed the details of what had happened while she was sick. Apparently, Hakonsson had had the foresight to have Thrand lure Loftur away from the Braksson steading to keep him from learning of Hekla's blatant disregard of his orders. Guilt twinged in her stomach, but as Sigrún updated her on the progression—or lack of progression—of the job, the feeling quickly dissolved.

It seemed while Hekla was unconscious, everyone had examined the site of the third attack. Not once did they venture into the woods, nor had they searched the borderlands for markings on the trees.

According to Sigrún, Eyvind and his men were raucous participants in the Winter Nights celebrations. While Konal and Loftur were content to lounge in the seats of honor, Eyvind and his retinue participated in drinking competitions and arm-wrestling matches with an increasingly ridiculous set of wagers. During one memorable loss, Onund Ale Drinker had had to strip naked in the middle of the Hungry Blade and run down Istré's central road. During another, Thrand had dropped to one knee before one of the Old Mothers and recited terrible poetry.

Thank the gods the double black moon nears, Sigrún continued. *The end of these celebrations cannot come soon enough.*

At mention of the double black moon, the hairs on Hekla's neck lifted. She couldn't help but think of that dream—of the mist seeping through the walls and into Istré. And while Hekla was not one to put weight on dreams, it felt like an ominous message.

She forced herself to drain her cup. Whatever was in that tea, it was doing good work, enlivening her blood and melting her exhaustion away. Hekla pulled the furs from her lap, then placed her feet onto the floor. After waiting a moment for the lights in her vision to clear, she gingerly stood.

Sigrún watched her warily. *You should rest.*

"I've rested enough already. Besides, I cannot hide away in bed. You know well enough how it is."

Hekla didn't need to spell it out. The pair of them had the double disadvantage of being female *and* disabled. A single sign of weakness, and any respect they'd managed to grasp for themselves would be gone in an instant. Women like Hekla and Sigrún had to be perfect all the damn time. And in moments like this, it was utterly exhausting.

Sigrún's jaw hardened, but she nodded.

After Hekla had dressed and twisted her prosthesis onto its metal anchor, she and Sigrún made their way down to the Hungry Blade. The mead hall was packed to the brim, a wall of noise crashing upon them as they entered. Candlelight guttered down from iron chandeliers, catching on the tapestries and weapons mounted to the walls. Bodies jostled about as ale sloshed and dice clacked across the tables. Hekla caught sight of Halldora, a strained look on the barmaid's face as she scurried among warriors, refreshing their cups with a jug of ale.

Her gaze fell to the high seats, and she scowled. There sat Loftur, clad in layers of silk, a crown of woven barley askew on his head. Beside him, Konal rumbled with laughter before tossing back ale from a golden goblet.

But a roar from the central long table quickly diverted her attention. Hekla's scowl only deepened. Eyvind Hakonsson's arm was wrapped around Thrand Long Sword's shoulder, the pair's eyes closed as they swayed and sang a bawdy tune. Tonight, the top and sides of Eyvind's hair were coiled into tight tracks, woven into a set of larger braids spilling down his back and around his shoulders.

She caught sight of the pair across from Eyvind and blinked. Onund Ale Drinker danced with Alf the Slender, who seemed to be wearing an apron dress.

What in the eternal fucking fires was going on here?

The song ended, Alf the Slender taking a bow as those around him erupted in cheers and whistles.

"A rematch!" he bellowed, climbing back onto the bench. Across the table, Eyvind was already throwing his braids over his shoulder, positioning his elbow to arm-wrestle Alf. A barmaid slunk up behind Eyvind, slender fingers massaging his shoulders as she bent low and whispered in his ear.

As though sensing an impending storm, Sigrún tugged on Hekla's sleeve, then signed, *I'll find us a seat while you talk to Hakonsson*.

Hekla nodded and fought her way through the mass of bodies before she could think twice.

The moment Eyvind caught sight of Hekla, he shot to his

feet, his expression morphing from dazedly drunk to enraged. Eyvind stormed toward her, shoving a drunken warrior out of his way.

He was angry at *her*? Hekla's hand curled into a fist.

But a large body collided with hers from the left. Had she been of sound mind, Hekla would have sensed it coming and would have easily dodged it. But the fever's lingering effects had left her off-kilter, and she staggered sideways. Suddenly Eyvind was beside her, one arm slipped around her waist, the other deflecting the bulk of the warrior's momentum.

"Your bed calls to you, Bersi Hairy Cheeks," Eyvind told the culprit.

After mumbling a nearly incoherent apology, the man—whom Hekla did not recognize—stumbled toward the mead hall's doorway.

"How is it that you already know the names of each resident of this gods-forsaken place?" Hekla grumbled, shaking herself loose from Eyvind.

The mischievous glint she was used to seeing in Eyvind's eyes was nowhere to be seen. "What are you doing out of bed?" he demanded.

"I—what?" Hekla blinked, taken aback at how legible his words were. A moment ago, she'd thought him drunk, but now it was clear he was completely sober. "I'm *fine,* Hakonsson."

"You need to rest. You almost *died.* It's a miracle you're even alive—"

"'Twas only a fever."

"It wasn't a *fever,* you infernal woman, it was that bloody gods-damned mist." Eyvind glanced over his shoulder. "I cannot have Loftur dissecting our every word from across the hall." Guiding her by her prosthetic's elbow, he directed them to the back exit of the mead hall and into the alcove linking the hall to the inn.

It took Hekla's eyes a moment to adjust to the darkness, but when they did, she was keenly aware of how small the space was. "Have you investigated the staves?"

She could *feel* his glare despite the darkness. "Rushing into those woods all by yourself?" he said, ignoring her question altogether. "Why would you do such a thing? I do not understand why you would risk yourself so recklessly!"

Her brows snapped together. Did the man understand nothing of what this job meant?

"You look better," he continued, his voice softening. "Your cheeks have some color to them. But I see you're not quite steady on your feet yet. Did you drink the tea the healer left?"

Hekla blinked at the sudden change in direction. "Staves, Hakonsson. Focus. Have you followed the Spiral Staves?"

Eyvind opened his mouth, then closed it.

"I gather that's a no. Never mind it. You can continue to cavort about, while Sigrún, Gunnar, and I—"

"You will *not* go back in those woods." Eyvind raked a hand down his face. It was a boyish gesture, one that, much to her chagrin, dampened Hekla's anger just a touch. "I cannot have you defying my orders. Our duty is to complete this job while honoring Loftur's—"

"Our *duty* is to the people of Istré."

"Precisely! And it's a miracle I was able to keep your insolent act from Loftur. Next time, I mightn't be so fortunate.

But Konal and some of my warriors . . ." Eyvind laughed, though he sounded far from amused. "Your defiance weakens me in my men's eyes. If it were anyone else, they'd be cast out from my retinue."

Hekla folded her arms over her chest, daring him to say what he was dancing around.

"But as a favor to you," Eyvind continued, "I'll allow you a second chance."

The laugh that fell from her was far from amused. "A second chance," she repeated numbly. Of all the words he might have chosen . . .

"Hekla," Eyvind whispered, his hand sliding behind her left elbow in a move that seemed meant to steady her. For a moment, Hekla forgot. Swayed toward him. Then her senses swarmed back, and she yanked her arm free.

Eyvind blinked, as though he, too, had forgotten. He cleared his throat, but when he next spoke, his voice was still a little rough. "I can only give you one more chance, Hekla. If you disobey me again, I'll have you carted back to Kopa."

Her former husband's voice invaded her mind, his words still fresh despite the years gone by.

I'll cart you back to the house. Cuff you to the post. Then you'll learn not to disobey your husband.

Hekla's anger erupted like hot lava, eager to scorch and destroy. She pushed off the wall. Brought her face level with Eyvind's. "Try to cart me anywhere, golden boy, and I'll tear the guts from your body."

And with that, she spun on her heel. Ignoring the stars dancing in her vision, Hekla stormed back into the mead hall in search of Sigrún.

CHAPTER ELEVEN

Days Before

Hekla moaned so loudly she was certain they could hear her in the stars high above. Yet she couldn't bring herself to care—not when she straddled the Fox's face. Not when he gripped her trembling thighs, holding her to his mouth as he worked her sensitive flesh. And as the pleasure that had been coiling ever tighter in her belly burst at last, nothing else mattered. Magenta and saffron bloomed in her vision, a kaleidoscope of spinning, melting shapes, as her palate was coated with the taste of sweet angelica and honey.

Utterly wrung out, Hekla half rolled, half tumbled off the Fox. They'd started end-to-end, yet at some point, she'd abandoned his cock entirely. As she panted on the blanket, the world seemed to swell around her. But as a stinging slap landed on her arse, she was yanked back into reality.

Hekla scowled up at the Fox. Propped on an elbow, he grinned back at her with pure male arrogance. But as his gaze roamed over the curves of her body, it shifted to something intense and unreadable. As it skimmed over her residual limb, she braced herself for the questions. But he only said, "You look beautiful like this."

She frowned. "You're mocking me."

The Fox's brows dipped low. "I'm not."

Hekla searched his face for amusement or mockery but was startled to find genuine confusion.

"Let us try this again," he said, sliding a finger along her lower lip. "I'll tell you you're beautiful like this, bathed in moonlight with your cheeks flushed, and you'll accept the compliment." The Fox leaned down and pressed his lips against hers, the kiss quickly devolving into a deep, lush thing. Much to her chagrin, Hekla found her left hand hooking around the Fox's nape, pulling him closer. She was dimly aware that this man had far too much power over her—that he was the kind of danger she'd worked so hard to avoid.

But the needy sound from deep in his throat wiped all such thoughts aside. His desire for her was clear as daylight. And as he drew back, he rested his forehead against hers, his eyes filled with that same intensity.

"You understand now, don't you?" The Fox's breaths were ragged, a sharp edge to his words. "I would never jest about such a thing."

And with that, he rolled away, leaving Hekla blinking up at the star-filled skies. Who in the gods' sacred ashes was this man?

She struggled to a sitting position, glad to see that all intensity had faded from the Fox's eyes. He puffed his chest out and loudly proclaimed, "Another round to the Fox!" His smile only widened as he took in Hekla's expression. "Oh, don't be so grim. It's not as though you, too, didn't win a prize."

"Gods. How did I find the largest of all man-babies in the realm?"

He snorted. "Do not lament the fact that you are so sensitive to my touch, Lynx. I like this about you. A weakness in your tough armor."

Hekla looked away to conceal her discomfort, but the Fox did not miss the shiver that rolled down her spine.

"You're cold." He found the spare blanket and bundled it around their shoulders. He arranged himself beside her, and they sat side by side, staring at the rushing river. It was impossible to miss that the warrior had not found his own release, but when he caught her looking, he smirked. "You can try again when you're warmed."

She fought the urge to elbow him in the ribs, but instead leaned into his heat. The Fox took her cold left hand between his, rubbing warmth back into it. Hekla's insides warred; one part cringed away from such overt affection, while another reveled in the comfort that came from his ministrations.

As they sat in silence and the Fox readjusted the blanket to cover her thighs, Hekla's thoughts drifted maddeningly to Loftur. *Gods.* How could she be thinking of him at a time such as this? But more infuriating, how could the witless man still refuse her entry to the woods? Did he truly think they could defeat the mist without identifying its origins?

The Fox had folded her right leg over his lap and was now massaging her foot. "What consumes your thoughts?" he asked, thumbs digging into the arch of her foot. It felt so good she nearly groaned.

"The cod-brained man I work for—"

The Fox's thumb dug in sharply, causing Hekla to break off with a yelp. Her glare was met with a look of amusement. "'Tis a waste of a beautiful night to have your mind in a different place."

As his fingers resumed their gentle motions, Hekla realized he was right. When she was thinking of the job, she missed the beauty surrounding her—moonlight gleaming off the river waters, the trill of a winterwing from somewhere nearby.

"I wasn't always like this," she murmured, more to herself than to the man beside her.

"What do you mean?"

She hummed softly. "I used to . . . take joy in the small things. Dream about the future."

"And now?"

"Now I . . ." Hekla sighed. "My thoughts often drift to things that have come to pass."

"Good things, I hope?" said the Fox. The innuendo in his voice was impossible to miss.

Hekla allowed her gaze to roam along the warrior's long limbs and became acutely aware of each place they touched.

"*Now* what is going through that beautiful mind of yours, Lynx?" asked the Fox with a chuckle.

"I'm wondering," she said, sliding a finger along the jagged red scar on his shoulder, "what kind of weapon did this to you?"

The Fox craned his neck to examine the scar, and when his eyes met hers, they were filled with mischief. "I had a run-in with a tree."

"A tree?"

"Aye. It had the nerve to grow from the side of a cliff."

Hekla's brows drew together.

The man chuckled, smoothing a thumb along the scar. "There is a cliff overlooking my favorite swimming hole. A friend of mine dared me to jump off it, and well, as I've said, I never lose—"

"So, this wound is wrought of male pride." Hekla scoffed. To her own surprise, she leaned forward and pressed a soft kiss to it.

The Fox looked delighted, and there was something so . . . pure about his smile. "The tree doggedly tried to thwart my fall, but I am pleased to say I prevailed."

Hekla shook her head with silent laughter.

"And this one," the Fox said eagerly, showing her the scar on his inner wrist, "was acquired after drinking too much ale at my brother's birthday feast and tumbling down the privy stairs."

Hekla took his wrist in her hand and kissed the scar in question.

"And this one"—the Fox threw the blanket back and twisted to reveal a mark etched into the side of his torso—"was also acquired after drinking too much at a feast."

Hekla leaned closer, letting the scent of him permeate her senses. "That's no scar," she teased. "'Tis a tattoo. And a terrible one at that. What is it meant to be?"

"A dragon. Can you not tell?"

Hekla truly could not. Chuckling, she kissed the tattoo all the same. "I see you have a rather reckless streak to you."

"You see reckless, I see *living*."

Hekla straightened and peered into his eyes. "Do you never regret your choices? Wish you could go back and be smarter?"

He shook his head.

"If I'm to understand," said Hekla slowly, "you're a man who lives in the present, perhaps without considering the future. And I'm a woman whose mind dwells on the past."

The Fox's gaze grew thoughtful. "It would seem that way."

An incredulous laugh fell from her lips. "I want to be more like you tonight," said Hekla impulsively.

A hint of a frown marred his beautiful face. "Are you—"

"Teach me."

The Fox contemplated silently for a moment. "You can start by . . . sharing a secret with me."

It was not what she'd been expecting. "A secret?" Hekla scowled. "And how do I know you're not digging for information?"

He shrugged. "I suppose you'll have to trust me, Lynx."

Hekla's old instincts urged caution, urged her not to trust this man, but as she stole a glance at him, she found herself saying, "I taste colors."

The Fox laughed, then stilled. "You taste—"

"Colors. When I find pleasure."

The Fox's pupils spread like ink through water. When he spoke, his voice was rough as sand. "Explain."

Hekla wanted to retreat inside herself—to erect her sharp defenses meant to keep others out. But there was something special about this night, this riverbank, this man. And strangely enough, her revelation made her feel momentarily free from both the past and the future.

"Violet tastes like strawberries," she said. "Gold is a bitter, aged mead. And magenta . . . magenta tastes like honey." Hekla buzzed in the wake of this confession—a secret she'd not even told Rothna when she was madly in love with him.

Hazel eyes watched her from beneath sweeping black lashes. "What color did you *see* just now?"

"Magenta."

"Magenta," repeated the Fox, in a low, deep voice. He cleared his throat. "I've never heard of such a thing." He rubbed his beard, deep in thought. "I need something good to match your truth." He was silent for a long moment, before saying, "I hope that second chances are a very real thing."

"Ah," said Hekla, watching him carefully. "So, you do have regrets after all."

The Fox's sigh was heavy. "Only this one thing."

His words held a melancholy that Hekla did not care for. "Second chances *are* a real thing," she found herself saying. "I'm living proof of it." She did not have to show him her prosthetic arm for the Fox to glean her meaning.

Hekla braced for the inevitable slew of questions that would follow and mentally flipped through the false answers she usually gave her paramours. She'd learned long ago that nothing dampened the mood like discovering that her former husband had chopped off her arm and left her for dead.

But the Fox only threw her a grateful smile. "Let me try a better truth," he said, his face contorting in mock contemplation. "I only pretend to like ale."

Hekla could not help but smile at that. "Pretend?"

"Why a warrior is expected to drink something that, quite frankly, tastes like urine, I do not know."

The corners of Hekla's lips tipped up. "And what of brennsa?"

The Fox's eyes widened in false alarm. "Never again. One home set alight is enough—"

Hekla's head fell back as laughter burst free. "There's a story here, I'm certain."

"Aye, there is," said the Fox. He turned toward her, eyes so dark only a thin strip of hazel remained. "But I'd rather discover what the color *green* tastes like."

Hekla's lips met the Fox's. And as his hand skimmed along her waist, she knew she was going to lose yet another match.

CHAPTER TWELVE

Present Day

Hekla dreamed of weathered-timber beams groaning in the wind—of chains clanking against the twin oak doors of a barn. It was utterly dark. A moonless night. Stunted fields of barley quivered all around her, and the tall spindly pines of the Western Woods swayed. The setting was familiar, yet the lone apple tree in the middle of the yard was distinct, and Hekla was certain she'd never laid eyes on this farm before.

A heartbeat began low and deep within the woods, but time was slippery in this land of dreams, and soon it thundered in her skull. White tendrils slunk from beneath dead shrubs, from behind gnarled trunks, and Hekla could feel the mist's longing—could taste its hunger as it glided through the grass toward the barn.

She opened her mouth to scream a warning, but no sound came. Hekla watched helplessly as the mist seeped between the boards of the barn. Screams rose from within, joining the hammering beat of the mist in a chorus of agony, man, woman, *child*.

Hekla had to help them, had to make it stop, but she did not know how to best this enemy. A large form bounded into her vision, shaggy tail twitching. *Wake,* it said.

Hekla sat up with a gasp.

Her heart raced, and cold sweat misted her brow. The dream had been so vivid and felt so real.

Not real, she told herself, trying to banish the sight of that barn from her mind. *You are in your chambers.*

The sounds of the Winter Nights' celebrations had faded away, and the faint light blooming from beneath the window coverings suggested that dawn neared. Hekla drained her waterskin. Sleep would not find her, not after a dream like that, and so she pulled the furs aside and dressed for the day.

Today her legs felt a bit steadier, the ache in her skull not quite as sharp. Hekla ate a few strips of dried elk, then grabbed her gear and made her way to the yard behind the Hungry Blade.

The horizon was brightening, casting just enough light for Hekla to see she was not alone in the yard. The figure across the courtyard worked through a series of rapid sword thrusts before sinking into a quick defensive stance. Her stomach clenched tight; she knew those movements. Had faced them before.

Hekla supposed she should not be surprised to find Eyvind Hakonsson up before the sun, diligently working through a defensive routine.

I hope that second chances are a very real thing.

The Fox's words from their night together rang in her ears, and Hekla gritted her teeth. *This job* was the Fox's second chance, and the realization curdled the last vestiges of her hope. The man would not squander it, which meant he would do as his father ordered.

As a favor to you, I'll allow you a second chance.

Eyvind's remembered words from last night kindled her anger to life.

Fuck him.

Fuck every patronizing man who disregarded her opinion because she lacked a certain appendage. Who brushed off her passion and called her *temperamental*. Who told her to smile, as though she needed to change herself to put them at ease.

Fuck them all.

Hekla stripped off her cloak and began working through movements to loosen her body. She refused to grant Eyvind so much as a glance, even when she felt his eyes on her. Thankfully, he had the good sense not to try to talk to her as Hekla channeled her anger into her routine. Best to get it all out here now, in the sparring grounds, so she would not do or say something regrettable later. She could not help Istré's citizens if she were ousted from the job.

By the end of her routine, sunlight streamed over the stable's roof and steam rose from Hekla's sweat-slicked skin. Roosters crowed and hooves clopped, a squirrel darting along the fence.

Hekla froze.

The creature paused on a fencepost, one paw lifted as it listened for predators.

Just a squirrel, bjáni. Hekla forced her attention to her waterskin, refusing to so much as glance the creature's way as she took a long drink.

After gathering her gear, she sauntered into the mead hall. Eyvind's men lined the benches, talking among themselves. Hekla ignored the occasional scowl sent her way, but her ears pricked up as she caught a wisp of conversation.

"Konal had best loosen the leash." It was one of Eyvind's warriors.

Hekla slowed her stroll.

"It's not a good look for Eyvind, having to heel to Dear Papa's every command."

"Least we're out of the city. Another patrol of that wall, and I'd gouge my bloody eyes out." This came from a rangy man with red hair fastened into a warrior's braid.

The first warrior grunted his agreement. "Do you really think Konal's ritual will help?"

The red-haired warrior shrugged. "Suppose there's only one way to find out."

The first man opened his mouth to reply but caught sight of Hekla and glared. With a mocking salute, Hekla ambled on, but her mind spun at what she'd heard. So, *this* was Konal's business here? What was this ritual the warriors spoke of, and why had she not been informed of it?

Put together with the fact that Jarl Hakon was an old friend of Loftur's, it didn't take a genius to figure out what was happening here. Jarl-bloody-Hakon had sent Konal to do something on Loftur's behalf. The *jarl* was trying to control things from Kopa. No wonder they were making no progress!

Gods, what a mess.

Gunnar waved her over to an empty bench space. "Feeling well enough to spar, are you?" He nudged a plate toward her.

Hekla's eyes narrowed on the stack of oatcakes generously drizzled with honey. "What's this for?"

"The daymeal." Gunnar shrugged.

Hekla was no fool—the man had never fixed a plate of food for her in his life, which meant he was angling for something. But Hekla was too hungry to care. Hunching over her plate, she wolfed down her meal like she hadn't eaten in days. Which, she supposed, she hadn't.

"I could spar with you tomorrow, if you'd like."

Hekla's knife paused in midair, and she assessed Gunnar from the corner of her eye. This man had been the last member of the Bloodaxe Crew to rise in the morning for *years*. Was he unwell? "Looking to get your arse handed to you before the daymeal, Fire Fist?"

He grimaced. "I suppose not. But we could"—he waggled his eyebrows—"*spar* in the evenings."

Hekla shook her head in amusement. "As subtle as a greataxe, aren't you?"

But a curious sensation twisted in her stomach. She and Gunnar had had a physical relationship for the better part of a year, and always, their expectations had been clear—sex only, no soft sentiments. Gunnar was a more than adequate lover, and over time, she'd even grown comfortable falling asleep in his bed. Yet the thought of bringing him to her furs suddenly felt unappealing.

Gunnar's arm slid around her shoulders, pulling her closer. "Is it flattery you want, Smasher? I can do that." His mouth was now right beside her ear. "I can do anything you'd like."

A prickling sensation rushed down her spine, and it was not due to Gunnar's proposition in the slightest. She turned to find a familiar figure in the doorway. Eyvind's ridiculous red cloak was bundled under his arm, his brow slicked with sweat. Her gaze met his, and her insides danced like a gaggle of little girls around a bonfire. A muscle feathered in Eyvind's jaw, but he strode past them and took his seat at Loftur's left.

Hekla exhaled and tried to gather her wits. She shook Gunnar's arm from her shoulder.

"I am glad you're feeling better, Fire Fist. But I'm afraid I must decline."

Hekla's head pounded in time to the hoofbeats as they made their way to examine a site where livestock had gone missing, but thankfully no human victims had been claimed. The sun was far too gods-damned bright, and Hakonsson's men far too cheerful. She watched the warrior who'd bad-mouthed Eyvind now speaking jovially to him. It didn't sit right with her, the way Eyvind's men had spoken of him behind his back. At least she'd had the bollocks to voice her discontent to his face.

Not your battle, she told herself.

Grinding her teeth together, Hekla tried not to wonder how this job would go were Axe Eyes here—were the Wolf and No Beard riding alongside them. She let out a long, weighted breath. There was no point in wondering. She had to make do with what she had.

They arrived at the farm when the sun was at its zenith. It was much like all the others—an abandoned longhouse; vacant animal pens; endless fields of stunted crops. A lone wagon sat stoically in the yard, and it was so gods-damned quiet, she wanted to scream.

Wincing against the drumbeat in her skull, Hekla dismounted and trailed the warriors into the stables. It was precisely as it had been when she'd last seen it: tools and hay strewn about, walls spattered with blood. Hekla stared at a scythe, somehow still leaning against the wall, as she breathed through the pain in her skull. It was strange how the world around this scythe could fall apart so completely, and there it still stood.

Follow me, came a shrill voice.

Hekla glanced around but found only Eyvind's retinue listening raptly to Loftur. She gave her head a shake. This gods-damned headache was truly doing a number on her. She tried to focus on Loftur as the chieftain relayed the events leading up to the grim discovery in this barn. But the voice flitted once more through her skull.

Protector must follow Kritka!

This time, she recognized the childlike voice. Hekla whirled, then locked her knees in place to prevent them from buckling. She blinked to clear her vision. But the squirrel perched on the barn's windowsill did not fade away.

"You. What are *you* doing here?"

We must go, said the voice.

"I'm going mad," Hekla mumbled. It was the only explanation.

The back of her neck prickled, and Hekla knew that Loftur had stopped talking. She winced, keenly aware that all eyes in the barn were now trained on her back. Someone tried to conceal a chuckle behind a cough, but it was enough to set her teeth on edge.

A figure appeared at her side, and she knew it was Eyvind even before he spoke. "You've pushed too hard too soon," he said softly, placing a hand on her shoulder. "You must return to the inn and rest."

Hekla's anger burned to life, and she shook his hand loose. "I only need some fresh air." And with that, she strode out of the barn.

The sunlight was bright, wreaking havoc on her throbbing skull. Hekla braced against the lone cart in the yard, drawing in long, calming breaths. Perhaps she ought to have listened to the healer and rested for longer. Because it seemed she was losing her gods-damned mind.

But she couldn't afford to look weak. Not here. Not with the eyes of all those male warriors upon her. Hekla needed to gather her wits before she did irreparable damage to her reputation.

Sigrún appeared beside her, that damnable black hood concealing her face.

What is going on with you? Hekla wanted to shout. *Why have you turned so nervous and flighty?* But then Hekla reminded herself a squirrel had just spoken to her. Clearly, she was not of sound mind.

The arrogant one watches, Sigrún signed.

Hekla straightened and followed her gaze, finding Thrand leaning casually against the barn doors. His face held a mixture of loathing and suspicion, and Hekla knew in an instant that Eyvind had assigned him to watch her. Did he think she would try to sneak back into the Western Woods? Did he not know the very sight of them sent a shiver down her spine?

Hekla turned away and gasped. "No." The gods-damned squirrel was bounding toward her. "You leave me alone."

Sigrún was signing, but Hekla was too distracted by the voice in her mind.

Protector, it said, *you must follow Kritka.*

"Leave me be, you insolent creature," she growled. But just like in the woods, the squirrel was unperturbed. It hopped onto the wagon, then scurried along the siding. Hekla's chest constricted as she looked into those beady black eyes. She saw intelligence. Saw more than a mere squirrel. She saw a grimwolf in the mist, keeping her from harm . . .

My mistress needs your help, said the squirrel, for Hekla was now certain it was the squirrel's voice in her head. *You must follow Kritka into the forest.*

Are you all right? signed Sigrún, concern etched into her shadowed face.

Hekla swallowed. "Can you . . . do you not hear that?"

Sigrún's brows furrowed. *Hear what?*

Hekla stole a glance at Thrand, whose stance was now anything but casual. He watched her with the keenness of a wolfhound who'd just scented blood.

Nothing, Hekla signed, hardening her jaw. Not waiting for Sigrún's reply, she whirled on her foot and took long strides toward her black mare. She had to get out of here. Get some rest.

Why do you not follow Kritka, Protector? asked the creature.

Hekla made the mistake of looking back; the gods-damned squirrel was following her. *My mistress begs of you—*

"Leave me alone!" exclaimed Hekla. She forced her voice to lower. "I do not know why you think I am this . . . Protector, but I can assure you I'm not." She raked a hand over her warrior's braid.

The squirrel cocked its head to the side, tail twitching.

"Leave me be!" Gods above, she was talking to a squirrel.

I will show you, said Kritka, whiskers twitching. *Kritka will help Protector see.*

"Not on your life," she muttered, refusing to glance back.

Hekla mounted her black mare and galloped down the road. She did not look back for a very long time. But when she did, she was eternally grateful not to see a squirrel bounding after her.

CHAPTER THIRTEEN

Hunched over her ale, Hekla tried to ignore the building chaos in the Hungry Blade. The Winter Nights celebrations seemed to start earlier and earlier each day. Already, Onund Ale Drinker was drinking straight from the jug, while Alf the Slender arm-wrestled one of the Old Mothers, and Halldora buzzed about looking completely frazzled.

Gunnar slid onto the bench beside Hekla, handing her a fresh horn. "I hear you're talking to woodland creatures now."

Hekla had returned from the steading an hour before the others. Had taken a long bath to try to clear her mind before channeling her nerves into another round of sparring practice. Thankfully, she hadn't caught sight of any suspicious-looking rodents.

Hekla accepted the horn and drank deeply.

Gunnar watched her carefully. "I also heard that kunta Thrand telling Konal you're not fit for this job. That you're a danger to yourself and to others."

A brittle laugh fell from her lips. "Did he now?"

Gunnar grunted. "But Hakonsson . . ."

She whirled on Gunnar. “Did he join in? Tell them I threatened to rip the guts from his body?”

Gunnar frowned. “Hakonsson *defended* you. Said you were the only one to survive the mist. That you were an asset to the team, not a liability.”

Hekla’s throat worked on a hard swallow.

Gunnar’s gaze slid around her face, assessing. “Tell me you did not threaten to disembowel our new ally and leader, Rib Smasher.”

She lifted a shoulder in a casual shrug.

Gunnar chortled. “Gods, but my girl is a violent one.”

Hekla’s gaze whipped toward him. “I’m not *your girl,* Fire Fist.”

The wide smile within his black beard told her she’d just reacted precisely how he’d expected. “Not yet.”

She scowled. “In case you’ve had the wits knocked from your skull, let me speak plainly. I am not your girl, Gunnar, nor will I ever be.”

But the lout’s smile only deepened. “Think about it, Hek. We know how to work together. We can trust each other. We know each other’s history.” His voice thickened. “And we know we work well in bed—”

Hekla shot him a look so scathing that Gunnar’s smile finally faltered. She opened her mouth to say it all—that she would never again be someone’s *girl,* that no man would ever have such control over her again. But before she could speak, a hand fell upon her shoulder.

“What?” spat Hekla, whirling around.

There stood Hakonsson, his jaw firmly set as he stared

down at her with those unnervingly beautiful eyes. She stared at the silver cuffs adorning his gleaming black braids, dumbstruck for a moment.

"Might I have a word?" Eyvind's gaze slid to Gunnar. "Alone?"

Gunnar's eyes met Hekla's, and she nodded. Grumbling, Fire Fist pushed to his feet and ambled away. Eyvind slid onto the bench beside her, then drank deeply from his horn of ale. She scoffed to herself. The man was a pretender; she knew for a fact that he didn't even *like* ale. But this near, Eyvind's irritating scent invaded her senses, transporting her back to what she'd thought was a night of freedom—when she was the *Lynx* and he was the *Fox*.

She felt his gaze on her and forced herself to meet it. Dark circles shadowed his eyes, as though this job weighed on his mind. A part of Hekla was glad to see it.

"What is it between you?" asked Eyvind.

Hekla blinked. "I—what?"

"You and Gunnar," said Eyvind, an unreadable expression upon his face. "What is it between you?"

"It is none of your concern."

His expression shifted, like a cloud drifting across the sun. A dry laugh fell from Eyvind's lips, and he soon took another long draught of ale. She ought to be angry—ought to remind him of their agreement to forget anything had ever happened between them.

But Hekla was reminded that Eyvind had stuck up for her in front of his men, which is why she quietly admitted, "I haven't been with him in quite some time."

Her words hung in the air, quiet and loud all at once. Just

like that night on the riverbank, Hekla felt firmly planted in the here and now. Why did he have this effect on her?

Eyvind raked a hand through his hair, his gaze growing distant. "There are concerns," he finally said, "about what happened at the farm today."

She should be glad he'd brought them back to *Hekla* and *Eyvind*. That he hadn't shared a truth of his own. Because Hekla didn't trust herself not to do something rash.

Still, the transition was so abrupt, it gave her whiplash.

"The . . . squirrel," Eyvind tried. "Will you tell me what startled you?"

A coarse laugh fell free. "I'm mad, isn't it obvious?"

"No," he replied, propping his chin on his fist and staring at her. "You can trust me, Hekla. Whatever you tell me stays between us."

Trust him. As she had that night by the riverbank. Hekla quickly rallied her defenses to do what they did best. "Trust you?" Her voice was a brittle thing. "When you haven't even told me the true reason for Konal's presence? Were you ever going to tell me he intends to perform some ritual?"

Eyvind's surprise quickly morphed into anger. "Where did you hear that?"

The swell of victory inside her felt false, but she'd come too far to turn back now. "Your warriors talk behind your back, Hakonsson. They likened you to a hound on Konal's leash. The red-haired one and the—" Hekla waved her hands.

"Vílki?"

She shrugged. "How should I know his name?"

His look was incredulous. "Perhaps because we've been here a week?"

Hekla leveled Eyvind with a look. "Focus, Hakonsson. Were I in your shoes, I'd make an example of them. Show them what happens to a warrior who slanders their leader."

He stared at her with open curiosity and wonder, as though she'd just revealed she was the queen of Íseldur. "What else would you do?"

"I would drop this absurd ritual Konal has planned and focus on venturing into the woods."

That snapped Eyvind from his reverie. "You must be patient. After the double black moon—"

"You're not listening to me, Hakonsson," she seethed.

"I hear you just fine."

Hekla's anger reached a sudden, violent boil. "If we wait until after the double black moon, we might all be dead!" she exclaimed, far louder than she'd meant. But Hekla could not shake that dream from her mind; the people in that barn, screaming as it engulfed them; Eyvind's eyes ember red as he succumbed to the mist.

Hekla met his gaze with her own unyielding glare. "Istré's people are not pawns in your games."

Eyvind's brows shot up. "I know that."

"Do you?" Hekla's heart pounded fiercely in her chest, and the words she'd pent up for days burst free. "You, who is granted the seat of honor beside Loftur simply because of your name? You, whose armor is so pristine, it's clear you've never been tried in battle? Not to mention you're a second son who clearly had no worries about being conscripted into the Klaernar's ranks. Did Dear Papa arrange that as well—"

"Bearing the Hakonsson name is not such a blessing as you might think," Eyvind snapped. It was such an uncharacteristic display of anger that it gave Hekla pause. "I do not expect you to understand." He growled in frustration. "You are the most maddening, hardheaded woman I've ever met." Eyvind's jaw shifted, but his eyes met hers. "Two days, Hekla. There are *two days* until Loftur's feast. Can you give me that?"

She pushed to her feet and folded her arms over her chest. Eyvind spun on the bench to face her.

"Two days," Hekla said with cutting calm. "Then I'm going into that forest, Hakonsson."

She didn't wait for him to answer. Hekla turned on her heel and left the mead hall.

Hekla dreamed of a land of dark shapes and shadows. A world of claws and sharp teeth. Of eyes ever watching and ears ever listening. She rode down the road, her legs bare against her mare's black coat. Beside her the forest gasped, desperate to free itself; but its world was controlled by a master, strings buried deep in the soil. And yet, beneath the spreading darkness in the woods, she could sense something else. Something quiet and ancient—a lone resistant being, protected by lignin's tough embrace.

Wake, said a voice. *We're here.*

Hekla's eyes flew open. Before her stood a farmyard. A barn, with double oak doors chained shut. Stunted fields of barley all around her.

And in the middle of the yard stood a lone apple tree.

She knew that apple tree—had seen that barn. Both were from her dream the night before. Hekla waited for the barn to whisk away, but gradually became aware of just how vivid this dream was. Had she been *cold* in her dreams before? Had she felt stones digging into her bare feet? Had she smelled that foul, moldering stench?

A nicker from behind had Hekla whirling. Her black mare chewed a mouthful of grass, watching Hekla impassively.

"Wake up," muttered Hekla, pinching her arm over and over. But despite the nips of pain, nothing changed.

The cold prickled her skin, and Hekla looked down to find her feet and legs bare. She was clad in naught but the long undertunic she'd worn to bed and her prosthetic arm, which she clearly remembered removing. What in the eternal fucking fires was going on? Had she sleepwalked here?

Sleep-rode-her-horse?

But where was *here*? Based on the chafing on her arse, she'd ridden some distance. And that single lonely apple tree identified this as the farm she'd dreamed about—the one with the people screaming in the barn as they were engulfed by mist. Her gaze landed on a heavy chain barring entry to the barn, and the cold in her bones deepened.

A small form bounded onto the path before her, beady black eyes glinting in the darkness.

Do you like Kritka's gift?

Hekla was past the point of fighting this delusion. She advanced on the squirrel, hands balled into fists. "What have you done? Where am I?"

Kritka brought you here, Protector, to help you understand the dark thing. Now you will trust in Kritka.

"Help me *understand*?" Hekla sputtered. "How . . . where . . ." The questions piled up too quickly for her to make sense of them. She was dreaming, and then . . . then she was here. "How did I come to be here?"

Kritka made your paws move many steps away from your burrow.

"Where are we, Kritka?" asked Hekla in a low growl.

The squirrel's tail vibrated in a happy sort of gesture, as though he preened at her use of his name. *We are at the burrow called Hagensson. Here, Protector will find answers about the bad thing. Then Protector will trust Kritka. Help free our mistress.*

"Hagensson," gasped Hekla, glancing toward the barn. This was the site of the first human victims—the farm Loftur had forbidden her to visit. Curiosity bristled inside her. "I shouldn't be here," she murmured, but her bare feet were already stepping toward the barn.

The sudden clank of chains sent a shiver down Hekla's spine, only heightening the eerie sense of having taken these steps before.

"You're awake," she reassured herself, then began reciting the information she knew of the Hagenssons to ease her nerves. "Site of the first human attack. Livestock vanished, the family noted missing when their eldest son failed to call upon the neighbor's girl."

Another gust of wind carried the unmistakable scent of rotting flesh, and Hekla's feet faltered. "Family of eight. Mother, father, four children, two grandparents. Only deep claw marks and blood spray found in their home—"

A grunt from within the barn brought Hekla to an abrupt halt. Her left hand reached instinctively for her sword, and she swore when she did not find it.

"Curse you, you bloody squirrel," she muttered. "Could you not have brought me fully dressed?"

The squirrel's nose twitched, and Hekla had the sense that the creature did not understand the concept of breeches nor boots.

"At least you had the good sense to put my arm on." Hekla unsheathed her claws, the reassuring glint of metal easing her pulse just a bit. But a long, low wail floated through the air, and the hairs on her arms stood on end. It was increasingly clear that something was locked inside the barn.

Before she could second-guess herself, Hekla took off at a brisk pace. She snatched an axe propped against the wall and used the butt to strike the metal padlock once, twice, three times. The sound rattled her eardrums and instantly agitated whatever was locked inside. A second screech joined the first, then a third . . . fourth . . . fifth . . . Hekla's nerves were on high alert, but she did not cease her assault on the lock.

You need fire, came the squirrel's voice, diverting her gaze away from the barn doors. Her gaze swung toward the creature perched upon what appeared to be a small bucket filled with unlit torches. And tucked just behind it, a firestone. Someone had left these here, but who, and more important, why?

Hekla soon held a lit torch in hand, allowing her to drive the axe into the padlock with far more accuracy. It wasn't long before it cracked open. Hekla shoved the door with her shoulder. The shrieks from within reached an earsplitting crescendo, rattling her bones.

Kritka will wait outside, chattered the squirrel.

Hekla sent him an irritated look, then lifted the torch,

casting light into the barn. The moldered stench hit her at once, making her eyes water, yet Hekla pushed through it and stepped inside. Her breath seized at what she found within. The Hagenssons, the Erikssons, the Brakkssons—all of the missing were here.

Except it was clear it was not *them* at all. Their flesh was a bluish gray, bruised and dripping black blood from multiple slash marks. Iron collars wrapped around their necks, and they were secured to the wall with chains long enough to allow movement. As two dozen faces swung toward her, Hekla flinched. They smiled too wide, their mouths filled with pointed teeth. But their eyes were the most frightening part of all.

Glowing red, like the embers of a fire.

A chill settled into Hekla's bones.

"Fuck," she muttered.

CHAPTER FOURTEEN

Hekla stood frozen, staring at the two dozen undead creatures before her. Between the blue tinge of their skin and the decaying flesh, she immediately knew the name for these monsters: draugur. The *restless dead,* some tales called them, though they were most often seen frightening off gravediggers—not chained up in a gods-damned barn.

Hadn't Kraki and his book ruled out draugur as the culprit for the mist? Yes, Hekla remembered. They'd thought draugur an unlikely cause for the mist and the missing people. But they had never considered that draugur could be *created* by the mist.

Long had she sought answers to the fate of the mist's human victims, and now she had them. They had indeed died, though they'd found no peace in death. Her gaze fell upon the long-taloned fingers, then to the deep, gouging wounds in several of the draugur. A story began to fit itself together—the mist Turned the first of its human victims, and the victims then attacked their own kin with those talons. It explained the blood, the deep gouge marks in the packed-earth floor.

Nausea churned in Hekla's stomach, and for a moment, she saw what might have been her fate in the Western Woods.

She recalled the feeling of the mist permeating her senses—as though it had sought the tethers of her life force and free will—before Kritka had come to her rescue.

The people in this barn had had no savior—no one to help them as the mist snapped through their threads and re-forged them anew. Staring at them, it was impossible not to notice the uncanny resemblance between the draugur in this barn and the forest walkers and red-eyed wolfspiders they'd fought on the Road of Bones. Putting all this together, it would seem the mist affected all living things.

"Why?" Hekla muttered. What could be the purpose of creating draugur? Why was the life force being pulled from the forest plants? Where did the mist come from, and how did the dead Klaernar and the Spiral Staves fit into the story?

The barn's tense silence broke as several of the creatures lunged forward with earsplitting shrieks. Hekla hefted her axe but held her ground, hoping those iron fetters held true. As the creatures reached the limits of their chains, the jangle of iron joined their riotous screeches.

Hekla was two paces away from their gnashing teeth, thankfully out of range of flying spittle. Holding the torch higher, she examined the creatures. Everywhere she looked were signs of humanity—reminders that these draugur had been people with lives and dreams. There was a tablet weave pattern around the collar of one draugur, and a string of amber and glass beads on a woman's apron dress. But when Hekla found a small carved horse nestled in the straw, her stomach churned violently.

Beside the toy horse, she found something altogether unexpected—the hindquarter of a deer, shockingly fresh.

"Someone has come to feed you," Hekla murmured. She spotted rumpled blankets. A pile of garments. "Someone has cared for you." Her mind whirled. Who had told her over and over that the human victims had vanished? Who had barred her from visiting this farm? It could only be one person. "Loftur did this."

Hekla had known Istré's chieftain was hiding things from her, but the scope of his deception left her aghast. Why would Loftur do this? Why would he hide this from her? But Hekla's chest clenched tight as Loftur's words flitted through her mind.

When Sunnvald is restored to His full strength, He will banish the mist and heal both our people and our lands.

Surely the man did not think his gods would save these people. That throwing a feast would cure them? Gods, but she didn't want to pity Loftur the Bloody Mutton Head, but Hekla had to admit, were she in his place—if it were her loved ones Turned undead—she might be desperate enough to try such a thing.

Hekla's gaze slid from draugur to draugur. Torchlight caught on long-taloned fingers as one beast clawed at its chains, trying to reach her. Near the deer carcass, one child-like draugur lunged at another, and they rolled across the ground in a tangle of chains and sharp teeth.

"You're already gone," Hekla murmured, sadness welling within her. "There's no coming back from this." The axe was heavy in her hand, and she yearned to grant the draugur the peace of a final death. But their existence was the proof she needed to convince Eyvind that Istré's chieftain was not of sound mind . . .

The clamor of chains came to an abrupt stop, every one of the draugur suddenly standing as still as stone. Those red eyes stared vacantly ahead, and a prickle of unease ran down Hekla's spine.

The head of the nearest draugur snapped to the side then came back up. And as Hekla stared into his glowing red eyes, she had the distinct sensation that a *new* presence peered out at her. The undead man cocked his head, examining her with unnerving intensity.

"You are not Loftur." His voice was raw and scraped, as though he had gravel trapped in his throat. Those red eyes slid all over Hekla with quick, jerky movements. "And yet you are familiar. Come closer so we can smell you."

"I think not." Hekla stared at the draugur, trying to understand. "Who are you?"

The undead man's nostrils flared. "You smell like her wolf."

The draugur's chin dipped as he looked at Hekla from under thick brows. "We have tasted you. You have great strength and would be an asset to our cause." A low hiss vibrated the air. "Come closer so we can finish what we started."

At the confirmation that she did, indeed, speak with the thing responsible for so much misery, Hekla tried for a smile, but she fell rather short. "Unfortunately for you, mist, you're chained to the wall."

"We will have you. We will finish what we started and bind your will to ours."

"What do you want?" Hekla demanded. "What is your purpose?"

"Purpose?" The thing seemed to consider her question.

"What is the word you mortals use?" The mist's avatar cocked its head to the side, and its voice deepened. "Feast. We will *feast*."

A cold pit opened in Hekla's stomach, but she had no time to consider it. A low, rhythmic pounding began beneath her feet, and the sound awakened bone-deep memories within her. It was screaming for help knowing no one would come . . . it was the slow drain of her life force as the thick white mist undulated all around her . . .

Those crimson orbs flared brighter. "That's right, mortal. Step closer and we shall finish the task quickly. Or you can try to run." The draugur's mouth widened in a jagged smile. "But it's already too late."

Hekla turned and stumbled out of the barn. Kritka leaped into her path, eyes wide.

Protector, take Kritka! pleaded the squirrel. Hekla bent low and let the rodent climb up and settle on her shoulder. And she *ran*.

"Too late!" came the draugur's voice, his laughter rattling like dry bones.

The mist's eerie heartbeat was already too fast, the ground beneath her rumbling with each pulsating beat. Hekla sprinted past the longhouse, but the black form of her horse was still too far away.

Protector won't make it, Hekla heard inside her skull.

"Can't you blast it away?" she asked, thinking of the grimwolf who'd saved her the last time.

Kritka used all our magic to get you here. Protector must use the fire!

Hekla looked down at the torch clasped in her metal hand; she'd forgotten that she still held it. The heartbeat was now a staccato coming from deep within the woods. Hekla lifted the torch, casting light upon the border of the woods, and recoiled in horror. The mist blasted through the trees like an angry squall. Frightened, Kritka burrowed his face into her neck.

Before, when she'd faced certain death, Hekla had felt a sense of peace and acceptance. Now she felt only anger. She finally had answers—finally had proof that Loftur was out of his bloody mind—and now those answers would die with her. But Hekla hadn't the time to dwell on any of it, because the mist was suddenly all around her. Kritka trembled on her shoulder, and Hekla drew a deep breath, bracing herself for the world of chaos she'd barely survived in the woods.

It never came.

The mist recoiled with an angry hiss as it neared her flaming torch. Hekla blinked, then gave the torch an experimental thrust forward. Again, the mist retreated.

Was she dreaming? The thick white mist had closed in on all sides, yet she and Kritka stood in a pocket of sorts. She looked up at the star-filled skies and realized that the mist could not pass above the flame. But she could sense its displeasure—could sense it probing for weakness as it swirled around them. Hekla held herself still and tried to trust that the torch would protect them. But the feel of this poison all around her—to be so near to a fate worse than death—was utterly unsettling.

Then everything happened in the span of a heartbeat.

The mist's attention withdrew, and it peeled away from Hekla and Kritka. Then it charged away like a cloud of angry wasps.

"What?" murmured Hekla, disoriented. Kritka clung to her, trembling like a leaf in rough autumn winds.

An equine scream split the air, and the blood drained from her face. Then she was running, feet pounding the packed-earth road as Kritka's claws gripped the flesh of her neck.

"No no no no no," she muttered, hoping, *praying,* she was wrong. The mist was now well beyond a hundred paces from the woods, yet it showed no signs of losing strength. It should have dissipated by now. Clearly, it was growing stronger.

Hekla cursed as a rock sliced into the sole of her foot, but she did not slow her pace. Her horse was now completely engulfed in mist, another high-pitched whinny increasing Hekla's urgency.

"Get back!" she screeched, waving her torch, now all but snuffed out. But she was too far. She was too late.

Emotion clogged Hekla's throat just as a cloud slid away from the moons. The sisters were the thinnest slivers of light, and as they were revealed, the air rattled with the mist's displeasure.

It happened so gradually that, at first, she wasn't certain it was happening at all. But after a minute, then two, the churning, wrathful cloud of mist was just a little more transparent. The mist was evaporating under the light of the sister moons. With each beat of her heart, the mist dissipated just a little more, until she could make out the black outline of a figure within.

But that was no horse within the mist. With misshapen limbs and a thick humped neck, *this* was a grotesque beast. And as glowing red eyes sliced through the haze, a shiver rattled Hekla's spine.

She extinguished her torch in the earth and pulled Kritka from her shoulder. "Go hide in the grass," she told the squirrel. Thankfully Kritka scampered off without complaint.

Hefting the axe in her left hand, Hekla unsheathed her claws on her right and advanced on the monster before her. The mist gave one last gasping breath before dissolving completely into the air.

"I'm sorry," she told her horse, stepping nearer. "I failed you."

Tears tried to push forth, but she would not let them free. Her insides rebelled at the task before her, but she thought of those pitiful draugur chained in the barn. Death was a mercy compared to such a fate.

Her horse charged at her, baring a maw full of teeth that were fit for a grimwolf. As the monster neared, a putrid, rotting stench swarmed up Hekla's nostrils, and her eyes watered. But she still managed to dodge the beast. As it passed, she stabbed her claws into the Turned horse's haunch and used the beast's momentum to swing herself onto the remnants of her saddle. Hekla swallowed the sob building in her throat and forced herself to do what must be done. She raised the axe high above her head and sliced it downward, burying it deep into its neck.

It should have been a lethal blow, yet the monster only reared in anger. The saddle strap tore through, sending Hekla hurtling to the side. Her body was airborne, but her claws were buried in the undead horse's flesh, and she used them to haul herself back. Hekla collided with the monster's flank, briefly knocking the wind from her chest. She clambered up, kicking the broken saddle off, and brought the axe back down with a cry of anguished rage.

With a growl that was anything but equine, the horse bucked wildly, trying to dislodge her. But Hekla's claws held her in place, and she brought the axe down again and again. The horse kicked with unnatural power, and once again, Hekla was airborne. This time, her claws pulled loose, and she careened through the air. She tucked her body, stalks of barley softening the blow as she rolled through her landing. Still, her shoulder crunched into the ground, and her metal arm jammed against her ribs. But Hekla hadn't the time to consider any injuries, as the Turned horse was once more charging at her.

She spun away with not a heartbeat to spare; lethal hooves gouged the earth where her head had been moments before. Its scent was nauseating, as was the bent angle at which its head now hung. From her position beneath the horse, Hekla could see she'd severed its neck more than halfway through.

She gathered her strength, a scream of fury and outright despair building inside her. Hekla slammed the axe into the underside of its neck, crunching into bone. Yet still the monster shrieked and reared up on its misshapen hind legs.

"Why won't you die?" bellowed Hekla. Hooves lashed down, and she rolled again, using her momentum to swing the axe upward. This time she felt the bone snap through. Black blood spurted from the wound, and at last, the monster showed signs of slowing. Breathing heavily, Hekla hauled herself to her feet and hefted her axe, before bringing it down on the wound with all of her strength. Her former horse stumbled to the side, then fell to the ground with earth-rumbling force.

“I’m sorry!” Hekla shouted, driving the axe down into the monster’s neck. “I’m sorry!” She repeated the words with each swing of the axe, until at last, the horse’s head came loose from its body.

The beast moved no more.

Her chest heaved, and she swiped tears and black blood from her face as she stared at the corpse of her faithful steed. Hekla fell to her knees. Slid her hands along her horse’s once-lustrous coat.

“Be at peace,” Hekla whispered, bowing her head.

CHAPTER FIFTEEN

By first light, Hekla's ribs throbbed viciously, yet inside, she was numb with exhaustion and disbelief. Hours had passed since she'd killed her Turned horse, and she could not push the sight of it from her mind. Those embered eyes and misshapen limbs would more than likely haunt her for some time.

Hours Hekla had walked, the sister moons and Kritka her only companions. The squirrel had been uncharacteristically quiet, and she suspected the night's terrible turn had not been part of his plans.

Hekla had discovered many horrors this night: the fate of the mist's human victims; the truth of Loftur's deception; the confirmation that the mist was, indeed, capable of Turning animals and humans alike. But she'd also discovered some things of hope; for one thing, the mist was repelled by fire. And moonlight—well, that had been even more surprising. The mist had evaporated before her very eyes.

Was this why the mist could not venture far from the woods? If it was vulnerable to moonlight, the forest's canopy might offer protection. But this thought only tightened the knots in Hekla's stomach, for Loftur's feast was slated for the night of the double black moon.

You're not Loftur, the mist had said through the draugur's mouth. At the time, Hekla hadn't thought anything of it. But now she couldn't shake it from her mind. Istré's chieftain had been communicating with that . . . *thing* in the woods. And it was suddenly clear that Loftur was not taking orders from Sunnvald at all.

What had the mist promised Loftur? That it would Turn the draugur in that barn back to their natural state? Was Loftur truly such an imbecile that he'd trust in something so obviously malevolent?

"Gods, but I want to throttle that man," Hekla growled, wincing as her bare foot landed once more on a sharp stone. But she frowned when her anger failed to materialize. Much to her chagrin, Hekla pitied Loftur. The man was truly an eel-head. Yet his heart was in the right place. He wanted to help those people. And as her mind's eye showed her the carved horse toy nestled in the straw—those childlike draugur wrestling in the barn—Hekla understood his motives entirely.

She also understood they could *not* hold a feast on the double black moon. In the absence of moonlight, the mist would not be restrained in the woods, and Istré's people would be ripe for the taking. There was only one logical plan of action: They had to evacuate the town.

Now Protector trusts Kritka, yes? the squirrel suddenly chattered in her mind. *Now Protector will come free our mistress?*

Hekla nearly groaned. How many times did she have to tell this squirrel she was not this so-called Protector? "I must return to Istré," she said aloud. "We must gather provisions and prepare to evacuate—"

The squirrel released a torrent of angry chitters before

scrambling down her body and scampering into the road. The rodent stood on its hind legs, glaring—if a squirrel could do such a thing—up at her.

Long Kritka has searched for the Protector. Kritka has been patient! The squirrel bared its teeth and screeched. *Protector must free our mistress!*

Hekla's shoulder was badly bruised, and she was covered in her undead horse's black blood. She was not in the mood to be screamed at by an unhinged squirrel. She opened her mouth to say as much, but the sound of hooves on the road diverted her attention. A figure appeared on the horizon. As the rising sun caught a swath of red, Hekla nearly fell to her knees in relief. She'd never been so gods-damned glad to see Eyvind and that ridiculous cloak of his. He urged his horse into a gallop, sending Kritka scampering off the road and vanishing into the shrubs.

"Good riddance," Hekla muttered.

Eyvind leaped from his horse and rushed toward her with startling speed. His eyes were wild, scanning her from head to toe, and then he was there, large, warm hands cupping her jaw and probing along her neck.

She swayed toward him but caught herself.

"Where are you hurt?"

"I'm fine, Hakonsson," she muttered, trying to extract herself, but those large, capable hands held her in place.

"Is that blood on your face?" His nose curled. "What is that smell?"

Hekla opened her mouth to reply, but as Eyvind's assessing hands reached her shoulder, she hissed in pain.

"You *are* hurt," he accused.

She finally managed to wrench free from his grip. "The blood is from my horse. It was Turned."

"Turned?" Eyvind glanced over his shoulder, and Hekla realized he was not alone. Thrand and Konal had appeared on the horizon, the rest of his retinue following.

"Listen," hissed Eyvind, "I don't have a lot of time. I need you to listen—"

"No, Eyvind, I need *you* to listen," Hekla shot back. "We must ride to the Hagenssons' steading. Loftur endangers all of Istré for the sake of the slain."

Eyvind's coal-black brows dipped low. "The Hagenssons' steading."

Hekla plowed onward. "Loftur has kept us from the Hagenssons' farm not because of a cleansing ritual, but because he keeps the mist's human victims chained up in the barn. But, Eyvind, they are no longer human. They are undead. The mist"—her voice broke at the thought of her horse—"it has transformed them into draugur."

Horses whinnied, and Hekla realized Konal and the rest of Eyvind's retinue had arrived, with Sigrún and Gunnar bringing up the rear. Eyvind's spine straightened, his gaze growing noticeably harder with their presence. Hekla glanced toward the warriors, her unease growing.

"Where have you been?" boomed Konal, dismounting in a single, smooth motion before storming toward them. "Good gods, woman, where are your breeches?"

Eyvind's gaze slid down Hekla's body, and he seemed to realize for the first time just how ill-equipped she was. A muscle in his jaw feathered, but he swiftly unclasped the pompous red cloak. Hekla didn't fight as he wrapped the cloak around her shoulders; she was too glad for the warmth and the coverage it provided. As Eyvind slid the cloak pin in place, imploring hazel eyes met hers. She sensed he was trying to convey something, but she hadn't the faintest inkling of what.

Hekla met Konal's hard gaze and held it. She was clad in naught but a tunic and Eyvind's cloak, yet she refused to cower. Refused to make herself smaller.

"Well, Eyvind?" growled Konal. "What has she to say for herself?"

"*She,*" ground out Hekla, "is right here."

Konal's steely eyes examined her. "You're at least two hours' walk from Istré, with no horse, no boots, smelling like the gods know what. And don't think it has slipped our notice that you've come from the direction of the Hagensson steading." He took a menacing step forward, but Eyvind's hand shot out, preventing him from taking another.

"Stand down, Konal," he said, the carefree, jovial man she'd come to know nowhere to be found. "Let me handle this."

Konal made a sound of frustration but retreated a few steps.

Eyvind closed his eyes and released a long breath. When he opened them, there was no softness to be found. "Tell me you did not disobey my orders and visit the Hagenssons' steading," he said slowly.

The fact that Eyvind was more worried about her venturing to the forbidden property than about the existence of two dozen undead creatures chained in the barn made Hekla's anger erupt violently. "All this time, Loftur has hidden vital information from us! They are *draugur,* Eyvind, and the fool thinks he can cure them by holding a feast—"

A muscle in Eyvind's jaw ticked, yet he showed no trace of surprise.

"You knew." Hekla took a step back in shock. Disbelief and hurt mingled in her chest, but her anger eclipsed them both. "I should have known! What are your father's orders?"

Eyvind's hazel eyes roamed her face. "Konal," he said, in a hoarse voice, "is schooled in the ancient rites of the old gods. My father has ordered him to perform these rites on the night of the double black moon, in order to heal those in the barn."

Laughter fell from her lips, a dry, brittle sound. "There is no healing those in the barn!" Hekla turned her gaze on Eyvind. "There is no coming back from what they've become. Surely you do not buy in to Loftur's madness? Surely your *father* is not such a fool—"

Konal clasped his hands behind his back, watching her with stern, dark eyes. "I'd watch what you say about Jarl Hakon, girl."

Hekla tried to swallow back her anger, yet her words came out sharper than she'd intended. "Loftur lies about Sunnvald coming to him in a dream. It is the mist. It speaks to him through the draugur in the barn. I do not know what it has promised him—"

"It's probably your moontime, isn't it?" said Konal coldly. He turned to Eyvind. "This is why I advise against women in your retinue."

With a low growl, Hekla unsheathed her claws and took a menacing step forward.

"Enough, Konal!" Eyvind exploded. For the span of a heartbeat, Hekla could have sworn she saw pure, untethered rage in his expression. But it was gone so quickly, she could not be certain.

As Konal stared at Eyvind, there was no mistaking the threat in his eyes. "Handle your business, son." And after a long, weighted look at Hekla, the aged warrior retreated.

Exhaustion and betrayal and grief twisted inside Hekla's skull. "You knew. You *knew* about the draugur. You let me toil on this job—let me *risk my life*—and all this time, you hid this from me."

Remorse flickered in his eyes, but it only drew her ire.

"What about *partnership,* Hakonsson? What about working together to defeat the mist?"

Eyvind released a heavy breath. "I wanted to tell you, Hekla, but your behavior has been erratic." Eyvind ran a hand along his braids. "Now everyone knows you've gone to the Hagenssons' steading after I strictly forbade it. You've pushed me into a corner, Hekla. There is no other way out."

Hekla braced herself for what was to come, but it hurt all the same.

"You're off the job." Again, there was that imploring look in Eyvind's eye that she did not understand. "I gave you a second chance, but, Hekla, there will not be a third. You must leave Istré immediately."

His voice was loud enough that all present could hear his words, and Hekla understood that his retinue was meant to witness this moment of dishonor. She should be angry—should be distraught—but the blasted numbness was back.

Hekla had no words. Instead she shouldered past him.

CHAPTER SIXTEEN

Several Days Earlier

Hekla's head thunked back against the door, a sigh of pleasure slipping from her lips. The coarse bristle of the Fox's beard scraped along the sensitive skin of her neck, but he soothed it with a lave of his tongue. In the dark hours of the night, time had ceased to matter, but at some point, both the Fox and Hekla had decided it would be far more comfortable to take their games to the bedchamber.

Which was how she now found herself pinned against the door, surrendering to his ministrations. The man knew just how to touch her to make all of her good sense flee her body. Raucous laughter burst from the stairwell. Hekla felt for the latch and swung the door open; it slammed against the wall, sending a tapestry crashing to the floor. As she and the warrior tumbled inside, Hekla managed to kick the door shut before the voices in the corridor reached them.

The room was dark and cool, and as the Fox tore his lips from her throat, Hekla made a plaintive noise.

"Ever impatient, aren't you, Lynx?" he murmured, walking backward with an arrogant smile. Gods, she wanted to wipe that smile from his face. Wanted to tear the sodden clothes from his body. But most of all, she wanted to win one round tonight.

Hekla admired the long lines of his body as the Fox added kindling to the banked fire in the hearth. Soon flames crackled high, and a dozen candles flickered through the room. Hekla simply stared at the Fox. Normally, she liked her men with a bit of grit to them—scars and calluses, toughened muscles earned on the battlefield. And as the light caught golden threading in the Fox's tunic and the splendor of his chambers, she had the sudden understanding that he was quite the opposite. Yet as he turned to her with hunger in his eyes, it didn't matter in the least.

They crashed into each other, lips colliding, fingers clawing wet tunics over their heads while they kicked off boots and breeches. Hekla twisted her prosthetic arm off, sighing as the wet, irritated skin around the metal joint was exposed to the air. The arm clattered somewhere on the floor, but Hekla could not care. Naked at last, they sank onto a fur rug right beside the hearth, too frantic to try to reach the bed. Hekla could not recall the last time she was so consumed with another, her mind so hazed with need. There was something about this man—the freedom in his laugh, the unrestrained way he touched and kissed—it reminded Hekla of something she'd lost long ago. And she was determined to recapture it through him, if only for tonight.

Soft furs slid along her back as the Fox rolled her over and loomed above her. Hekla froze for a fraction of a heartbeat. Then, with a burst of speed, she reversed their positions, rolling him onto his back while clambering on top.

"Like this," she purred, rising over his hips and sliding the hot length of him back and forth through her folds. Desire glazed his eyes as they raked over her body, his chest rising and falling with rapid breaths. Like this, Hekla felt powerful and in control; yet under his gaze, she felt something more: Beautiful. Whole. Unbroken.

She blinked the thought away and sank onto him. Her eyelids fluttered, a moan building in the back of her throat. Desire and longing had coiled tighter in her belly with each kiss they'd stolen on the way back from the riverbank. Now that he was inside her, stretching her deliciously, her desire was so potent she feared to move.

"You're going to lose," taunted the Fox.

"Won't," muttered Hekla, trying to get ahold of herself.

"Liar."

If goading her into action had been his plan, then the Fox had succeeded. Hekla planted her left hand on his chest and leveraged herself up before sliding slowly back down. Pleasure jolted up her spine as he slid along the perfect place inside her. Gritting her teeth, Hekla rode him as slowly as she could, trying to hold her pleasure at bay. Soon sweat slicked her brow, her body quivering and on the very brink of shattering.

The Fox sat up and cupped her jaw with one hand. "No, Lynx, don't come for me yet." His free hand cracked across her arse, the sting of pain yanking her back into the moment. Hekla glared at the arrogant smile. "There you are," he murmured, still cupping her jaw as he nudged upward, hitting the perfect place.

Helpless, her head fell back on a long, low moan. The edges of her vision blurred, the tension inside her coiling so tight it was nearly unbearable. On the brink of shameless begging, Hekla was almost glad for the next slap to her arse, wrenching her back from the edge. Gods, her pride couldn't take it if she lost to this man yet again . . .

"Not yet," he chided. His teeth nipped down on her earlobe, and she focused on the bite of pain. "I want to see how deep I can get."

The Fox held her in place as he bucked upward with increasing tempo, and Hekla widened her hips to accommodate the surge of him. He hummed his approval, grunted with pleasure, whispered filthy things into her ear. Hekla was dimly aware that the man's vocal nature only added to his appeal. To hear a man so unabashedly undone was a heady feeling. She wanted to tell him so, but she was barely hanging on—was too far gone to form words of her own.

"I want you to feel me tomorrow," he muttered against her neck. A hand slid into her hair, and he pulled her mouth to his in a deep, hot kiss. But as he drew back, she saw it in his blown pupils. In his corded neck. The Fox was close.

"Almost," he grunted, grasping her hips and pumping up—once, twice.

"F-fox!" Hekla moaned. She had the fleeting thought that it would be nice to know his true name, but then the edge was slipping through her fingers. Hekla was falling, spinning wildly, body quaking as a scream tore from her lungs. Scorching heat unspooled within her as her spine arched, and she spasmed around the Fox.

Like the northern lights dancing in the skies, vibrant green undulated across her vision. A spiced, earthen taste suffused through her body, all while the Fox's thrusts grew frantic. He stilled as he buried himself deep, groaning with such abandon that a fresh wave of green flowed in her vision. Those groans might be the most arousing sounds she'd ever heard in her life.

Her fingers dug into his shoulder, and convulsions rocked through her so fiercely, it was as though her mind was torn from her body and she looked down from above. They lay entangled on the furs, panting in unison beside the hearthfire. His finger pads skimmed gently along the notches of her spine, and Hekla frantically tried to come back to herself—tried to reassemble the far-flung fragments of her being.

How could this stranger wreak such pleasure from her body? She'd never come this hard in her life. Had never felt so thoroughly undone.

The Fox collapsed onto his back, pulling her with him and nestling her against his side. Good gods, the man wanted to cuddle. Her instincts told her to push away, yet her body was so lax . . . so completely boneless. Hekla closed her eyes. Let herself *be* for a moment.

The Fox traced lazy fingers along her collarbone. "I didn't hurt you, did I?" At her confusion, he clarified, "When you rolled us, I thought . . . you seemed to flinch."

Hekla chewed on her lip, considering her reply. Any other night, she'd have had a quick lie for him. Yet the Fox and his truths had given her such freedom that she couldn't stomach a lie in this moment.

"It is one of my rules," she murmured, looking up at his beautiful face. With his chiseled cheekbones and dark hair falling around his face, he was disconcertingly handsome.

"Rules?"

"No soft sentiments," she listed. "Do not spend the night. And I never let a man have power over me."

The warrior's thick brows drew together as he considered her words.

"If I'm on top," Hekla explained, "I'm in control."

That arrogant smirk was back. "I think we both know you were *not* in control—"

She covered his mouth with her left hand. "Quiet, Fox," she muttered with amusement. But voicing her rules made a hot, panicky feeling rise within her. She had her rules for more than her personal safety. It was for the preservation of her heart as well. She'd shared too much with this man—had given him too many pieces of herself.

"I should go," she said, sitting up suddenly.

"Stay," urged the Fox, fingers circling her left elbow. "Please."

Hekla closed her eyes. Tried to calm her racing heart. "I *need* to go."

"What did I say?"

Every muscle in her body wanted to lie back down, to settle against the man's heated skin. "It's not you, it's—" Hekla's panic sharpened into deadly points, and she whirled on the Fox, lashing out in desperation. "Aren't you going to ask me about my arm?"

The Fox's mouth opened, then closed, and for the first time in hours, Hekla felt like she'd gained the upper hand.

"Don't you want to know what happened to me? Don't you want to hear how my husband hacked my arm off with an axe then left me to die?"

Hekla flung the words at him, a last frantic attempt to

keep him away from her soft, vulnerable heart. She pushed to her feet, not daring to look behind her. Not wanting to see the moment the Fox recoiled like all the others. She snatched her tunic from the chair and scoured the room for her metal arm. She had to get out of here.

But the footfalls on the floorboards stilled her.

Eyvind took her wet tunic gently from her and pulled her against his chest. Hekla's restraint snapped, and she swayed into him, letting him wrap her in a tight embrace.

"Did you kill him?" he asked in a low and dangerous voice.

"Aye," she barely managed in reply.

"Good." His voice was rough, but his touch was so gentle, palms smoothing over her damp hair. Hekla reached for her rules, but they were nowhere to be found. The part of her she'd fought so hard to protect was now fully exposed, and she'd never felt so vulnerable in her life.

"I like you, Lynx," the Fox whispered into her hair. "I like that you say what you think. I admire your spirit. And you might be the most beautiful woman I've ever met."

A long, shuddering breath fell from Hekla, and this time, she didn't accuse him of mockery. This time, somehow, she felt it in the marrow of her bones.

"I will ask you one time, but you needn't answer. You're in charge."

Hekla wanted to laugh at the very concept, but she didn't have the energy.

"What color," said the Fox, "did you see just now?"

Hekla drew back with an incredulous look. "What?"

"When you found your pleasure. What color did you see?" His eyes were bright, dancing with laughter.

She bit down on her lip, her discomfort giving away to a soft, sultry feeling. “Green,” she admitted, smiling as his grin widened. “With a spiced taste. Something like róa.”

Gods, but she didn’t want to feed this man’s ego, yet she was grateful he’d brought them back to common ground. He entwined their fingers and guided her toward the bed.

Hekla could pull her hand free at any time—could retrieve her clothing and return to her own chambers. Yet she found herself following the Fox. Climbing onto the bed. Curling up against his side.

Only for a minute, she told herself.

“Since you shared a *real* truth with me, I ought to share mine with you.”

Surprise jostled through her. “You don’t have to.”

He glanced at her sidelong and smiled. “For some reason, I *want* to share with you. Perhaps you have sage wisdom to dispense.”

Hekla snorted, wondering if anyone had ever deemed her *sage*. “Very well.”

“Do you ever feel like no matter what you do, you’re not enough? It’s not enough?”

“Every gods-damned day,” Hekla muttered, thinking of Loftur.

The Fox exhaled, gaze drifting to the rafters. “My mother died while birthing me, and my father has never forgiven me for it.” He said it in a rush, as though each word pained him, and getting it out quickly lessened the agony.

“So perhaps,” he said softly, “all the scars you worshipped—”

“And the dragon.”

"And the dragon." His lips pulled into a smile. "Perhaps they weren't earned from a life well lived. Perhaps they were a plea for attention. An attempt to get my father to see me as more than the person who took his love away from him." Sadness filled the Fox's expression, and something inside Hekla woke up and growled.

His gaze suddenly shifted into a look of determination. "But I have been granted a second chance."

Hekla watched him carefully, trying to understand.

"My father has entrusted me with an important task. And when I complete it, he will see me as worthy."

"Fox," sighed Hekla. "You *are* worthy." Her fingers slid into his beard, and she drew his gaze toward her. "It is hard to learn that sometimes those we love most are undeserving."

He blinked and looked ready to argue, but she cut him off with the press of her lips. When the Fox drew back, she was glad to see no trace of sadness in his eyes.

"Break your rule," he whispered. "Spend the night with me."

A lump formed in her throat as Hekla's gaze bounced from one hazel eye to the other. "I can't," she whispered.

"Can," murmured the man, rolling onto his side and hauling her back against his chest. "You do it like this."

Hekla's heart hammered against her rib cage, her muscles rigid.

"Close your eyes," whispered the Fox, settling closer. Hekla did so, focusing on the heat of his chest behind her. Gradually, the tension in her body eased, her breaths slowing into rhythmic pulls.

She shouldn't stay the night. Knew she'd regret it. But for

once, Hekla couldn't bring herself to care. Sleep crept from the corners of her mind, and she found herself falling into darkness.

The last thought Hekla had before sleep consumed her was that though her rules were meant to keep her safe, perhaps they'd only shackled her.

CHAPTER SEVENTEEN

Present Day

Hekla stared bleary-eyed at the pair of saddlesacks laid out on her bed. Gunnar had gallantly shared his horse with Hekla, delivering her back to Istré, where she'd promptly requested bathwater delivered to her chambers. She'd sent Eyvind's red cloak to be washed and returned to him. Her hair was now clean, the putrid black blood thankfully scrubbed from her skin. Yet, Hekla could not seem to cleanse herself of the shame.

I gave you a second chance, but Hekla, there will not be a third. You must leave Istré immediately.

Eyvind's words were burned into her skin, but it was the eyes of his retinue that haunted her most. Every male warrior in his crew had witnessed her reprimand, and it as good as confirmed their every bias. She was an emotional woman, reckless and inept. And though Hekla had been fully covered by Eyvind's cloak, in that moment, she'd felt utterly bared.

Even remembering it now—that self-satisfied look in Konal's eye and the knowing glances shared among Eyvind's warriors—was enough to make her insides writhe in discomfort. Thrown from the job. Never in five years had she felt so powerless. Blood thundering in her ears, tears burning in her eyes, Hekla was back in that shed, her husband looming over her with the axe . . .

Hekla wrenched her prosthetic arm off and hurled it across the room. It slammed into the wall, then crashed to the floor. Immediately, her chest twinged with regret, but she ignored it and reached for her sword instead. With forced calmness, she laid it on her bed. The steel gleamed against the coarse wool fibers, and she allowed herself a moment to lament. This weapon was designed for the left hand, a rarity among warriors. It might take time for this sword to find a new wielder, but she was certain it would find one far worthier than she.

Was it wrong for Hekla to feel such relief that the Istré job was no longer her problem? She could unshackle herself from Loftur and his rules and liberate herself as leader of the Bloodaxe Crew. It was time to go back to worrying about herself.

"Done," she muttered. "I'm done." Hekla took one last look at her sword before turning to the door.

The door that was now bursting open. The door that Gunnar and Sigrún were now strolling casually through.

Gunnar's gaze fell on her prosthetic arm on the floor, and he raised an eyebrow. But the warrior did not ask about it as he collapsed into a chair and propped his feet on a stool. Instead, he said, "Well? What is the plan, Smasher?"

Hekla shot him a look of irritation before turning to Sigrún. The realization that the pair hadn't gone off with Eyvind and his retinue warmed her from within. But they knew well enough she'd been cast from the job.

Where do you need us? signed Sigrún, her brown eyes blazing. *It's clear you're the only one in these lands with brains in her skull. Hakonsson and his retinue are on Loftur's leash, which means it's only us standing between the people of Istré and the mist.*

Hekla stared at Sigrún and Gunnar; they watched her expectantly. How could they trust in her judgment after all that had happened?

"I don't know." Her voice was thin, so empty of conviction. She wanted to lie down. A brittle laugh escaped her, and she stared into the hearthfire. "Axe Eyes would know what to do."

"He's not here in body," said Gunnar. "But he's here in spirit. He's trained us all. So let us think like Axe Eyes."

Silence stretched out, disrupted only by the occasional snap of embers.

Hekla thought back to Rey, sitting tall upon Horse as they'd traveled the Road of Bones. *We'll survey the locations of the abductions and speak to locals,* he'd said. *We must observe this . . . mist. Determine if it is indeed cloaking creatures. We'll determine numbers, strength, formations, strategy, and then create a plan of attack.*

"We've scouted the attack locations," Hekla said slowly. "We've spoken to locals and observed the mist from inside and out. We have been blocked from examining how the mist is produced or where it emerges from within the woods." Hekla frowned. "But we have learned a few things. It is repelled by flame."

Gunnar and Sigrún exchanged a look.

"And we know the mist is not cloaking creatures," continued Hekla. "But rather is *creating* them."

What do you mean creating? signed Sigrún.

"My horse," Hekla forced out around a vicious wave of nausea. "The mist infected her, and changed her into something unnatural. I could not kill her the usual way—" Hekla let out a shaky breath. "I had to take off her head."

Gunnar toyed with a silver cuff on one of his locs. "So, this . . . *thing* . . . draws energy from the plants in the forest and uses it to create the mist, which, in turn, creates the undead creatures."

Hekla nodded. "And there is more. Tonight, I saw it; the mist was banished by moonlight. But on the double black moon—"

There will be no moonlight, Sigrún signed. *It will be able to venture unrestrained from the woods.*

"It seems there is no changing Loftur's mind about this feast," muttered Gunnar. "So we must plan around the festivities."

Evacuate in secret? signed Sigrún.

"Set a trap?" suggested Gunnar.

How many will attend the feast? signed Sigrún.

"I overheard Halldora mention gathering enough ale for two hundred," said Gunnar.

The trio looked at one another, and the determination in both Gunnar's and Sigrún's faces kindled hope in Hekla's chest. She did not have Eyvind, nor did she have the full force of the Bloodaxe Crew, but she had these two. And that counted for more than she could say.

"Three of us to protect and evacuate two hundred," murmured Hekla. It felt impossible, and yet, there was nothing to be done. Their task was set, and now they would see it through. Hekla pulled her warrior's mask into place, looking from her Bloodaxe brother to her Bloodaxe sister. "Do you trust me?"

They nodded.

"Good," she said, her resolve growing stronger with each beat of her heart. "Like Axe Eyes always said, *If you cannot trust the men and women beside you, you're already food for the corpse vultures*. And if we want to survive tonight, we'll need to remember that."

Hekla leaned in, beckoning the others closer. "I have a plan."

CHAPTER EIGHTEEN

As Hekla descended the crumbling riverbank, she glanced at the western horizon for the dozenth time that hour. No matter how often she reassured herself that twilight was many hours off, she could not help but check the sun's progress.

Tonight was the double black moon. Hekla's skin crawled as she imagined the mist waiting, watching, biding its time, while Istré's citizens bustled with excitement over tonight's feast.

Right now, casks of mead would be rolled into Istré's town square, and a boar roasted on the spit. The scant harvest of grain would be baked into griddlecakes and flatbreads and served with cheese, boiled eggs, and vegetables, all of which ought to be preserved for the impending long winter. Instead, this fare would be glutted upon in the hope that a long-slumbering god would save them from their foe.

Bitterness and anger wrenched in Hekla's stomach. A better person would hold compassion in her heart and know that Istré's citizens knew only the life they'd lived so far. And if these farmlands were anything like the ones she'd grown up on, they were ancestral lands passed down through generations. These were not just lands, but a part of their very identity. Of course Istré's citizens would want to believe in Loftur's plans, no matter how farfetched they were.

Hekla sighed, staring at the rushing waters of the river. She'd said all she could to those who would listen. Onund Ale Drinker had already been deep in his cups. Alf the Slender had looked at her as though she had two heads. Halldora alone had seemed swayed by Hekla's words, and she'd promised to gather what provisions she could.

Now, Hekla set her sights on tonight. This job was no longer about vanquishing the mist. Now, it was about saving as many lives as possible. This was bigger than her. Bigger than Eyvind Hakonsson's retinue. They'd need reinforcements. Clever minds to come together. But that was all in the future. If she survived tonight, that was.

Earlier, she'd made a great spectacle of riding from Istré on her new gelding, purchased from the blacksmith for more sólas than she cared to consider. Hekla had felt the eyes of Eyvind's men from atop the ramparts and smiled a secret smile. Little did Thrand Long Sword and the rest of them know, Hekla had steered her new horse off the road the moment she was out of sight.

And here she was a few minutes later, on the riverbank just upstream of Istré's culvert. With a deep breath, she plunged into the icy waters. The shock of the cold water thankfully soon receded, and she said a silent thanks for the specialized metal that made her arm so light—any of the older models she'd had would have been cumbersome and dangerous in these waters. With a deep breath, Hekla let the current pull her toward the culvert.

The stonework was even more remarkable up close.

Stone walls curled upward on either side of the river, channeling it through a narrow, circular passage. As the river was diverted into the waterway, and the sky above her was swallowed by stone, she tried to control her pulse. Gunnar had reported that the far end of the culvert was fitted with iron bars, and if all had gone to plan, he'd already cleaved through them with a specialized saw.

Hekla took a deep breath and pushed beneath the surface. The currents drove her into the bars, the strength of the river water pinning her in place. With great effort, she felt along the bars, searching for the cut space. Had Gunnar been detained? Unable to cut the bars? Her heart pounded harder as her lungs began to burn.

But then she felt the sharp edge of freshly sawed iron and silently thanked the gods. Hekla pushed herself through the gap, cursing inwardly as the top bar scraped along her bruised shoulder. Her lungs burned in earnest now, but it wasn't a moment later that the river's currents had delivered her safely beyond the culvert.

As her head broke the water's surface, Hekla gulped great mouthfuls of air and swam toward the shore. She could already see the hemp sack hanging on a scraggly bush. Inside, Gunnar would have left dry linens and clean clothes for her to pull on.

After clambering through the willows and onto the bank, Hekla didn't wait to catch her breath before shucking off her wet clothing. Soon she was dressed and pulling the hood of her cloak low on her brow.

She stole another glance at the sun, drifting ever nearer to the horizon.

"We're on schedule," she told herself, breaking a path through the bushes. "Gunnar and Sigrún will be foraging for supplies."

Hekla kept to the back roads as she crept through the village, preparing to note each wagon and horse as they passed. But her mouth was soon twisted into a frown. The miller's wagon was not sitting in its usual place behind the man's home. Nor was the wagon the armorer used to haul smelted ore. And the falconer's horse was not grazing in his yard.

Strange, she thought, pressing on.

Istré's town square came into view, and Hekla paused. In the distance, Konal and Loftur oversaw the erection of a pole, a banner bearing a sunburst flapping from high atop it. How long would Loftur continue this ruse? Hekla gave her head a shake and continued on her way.

It was risky to return to the yard behind the Hungry Blade so soon after leaving. But Gunnar had overheard that the near-empty stables had been offered to those hauling wagonloads in for the feast. Soon the peaked roof of the stables came into view, and it wasn't long before Hekla was crouched in the shadows of an empty stall. She peered through the slats, counting the wagons parked at the edge of the building. Voices carried from the yard.

"Is that all you have?"

The goosebumps from earlier rushed back as she recognized Eyvind's voice.

"Aye," came a woman's cautious reply. "I must wait until nightfall to risk taking any others—" It was Halldora.

Hekla repositioned herself for a better view into the yard just in time to see Halldora handing Eyvind the reins of a horse. As he led it to a hitching post, the horse's heavily filled saddlesacks came into view. Her gaze skipped to the three other horses secured at the post, and she cursed Eyvind Hakonsson for intercepting her supplies.

Hekla's mind swirled. She'd planned to use the inn's yard to store their provisions, but now Eyvind had made that impossible. Perhaps she could use the yard beside the blacksmith's, vacant after the family had fled Istré? But first, she'd have to lure Eyvind out of the inn's yard so she could steal the horses and wagons—

"Well?" Eyvind's voice had an unusual sharpness that made Hekla press her face back against the slats. Her lip curled as Thrand Long Sword sauntered into the yard.

"She's gone," said Thrand, scratching his close-cropped curls.

Something that looked an awful lot like worry crossed Eyvind's face.

"Vílki says she never rode past the checkpoint."

Fuck. Irritation stirred Hekla's blood. She ought to have known golden boy would have men watching her. Gods forbid Hekla interfere with their feasting. Shouldn't these eelheads be in the town square, brawling and singing and drinking ale from the jug?

"You can come out, Hekla."

Her brows snapped together. Eyvind was looking directly at the stables. A hot panicky feeling slid through her chest, but she wrestled it down and pulled her practiced bravado into place. Hekla pushed to her feet and strode from the stables with all the confidence she could muster.

Eyvind Bloody Hakonsson looked far too pretty. Tight

black braids wove along the sides of his skull, entwining with a looser large braid cresting over the top. The waning sun made the green in his hazel eyes shine ever brighter, and those lips she knew all too well were curved into an irritating smirk. "Thrand," he said, holding his palm out expectantly, never taking his eyes off Hekla.

Grumbling, Thrand fished coins from the purse secured to his belt and dropped them into Eyvind's outstretched hand.

Hekla folded her arms over her chest. "You're awfully pleased with yourself, golden boy."

"You just earned me twenty sólas by proving me right."

Now that she was in the yard, Hekla could better see the wagons; there were eight of them, each covered with a woolen blanket. With forced nonchalance, she strolled to the nearest and flipped the covering back. Here was the large wagon the armorer used to haul smelted ore, but now it held the kind of lifesaving provisions the Bloodaxe Crew had once carried: a tinderbox, crates of dried meats, waterskins filled with water. Hekla's gaze slid to the next wagon, its vibrant blue wheels marking it as the miller's. It was beginning to look like Hakonsson was preparing for an evacuation.

Her heart pounded, chest filling with hope. Could it truly be? She could not come up with any other explanation for the provisions now gathered here in the yard. But with that hope came the sharp pang of yet more deception.

"Why?" she asked, without turning around. She could not let him see the pain on her face. "Why did you brush aside my warnings? Why did you belittle me before your men?"

She heard him take a step forward.

"I tried to tell you." There was remorse in his voice, but it did little to ease her pain. "Then Konal arrived and discovered you'd been to the Hagensson steading and"—his exhale was weighted—"I had no choice but to send you away. I'm only glad you proved me right by sneaking back in."

"You listened to me," Hekla murmured. Eyvind had been listening to her all this time. He had come through—had heeded her warnings. But only after throwing her to the wolves.

"Sending you away bought us some time to prepare for an evacuation. Konal and Loftur's defenses are lowered; they're busy preparing for the feasting rituals."

Hekla nodded, hating the burn in her throat. She gathered her strength and turned to face him. Clad in his pompous red cloak and with the finest of weapons belted at his hips, he looked every bit the jarl's son.

"Your second chance," she said sadly, realizing all that Eyvind prepared to sacrifice. There would be no redemption in Jarl Hakon's eyes once he learned that his son had deceived Konal and Loftur. "You've done the right thing," she said in a voice of steel, and she meant it. She was proud of him. Sadness panged through her with sudden intensity. What she wouldn't give to go back to that night when he had been the Fox and she the Lynx.

But it was only ever an illusion.

Eyvind glanced at Thrand then back to Hekla. "Hekla, I—"

"Don't worry yourself, Hakonsson," said Hekla. "You did what any good leader would do in that situation. I understand well enough."

Hekla put her hands on her hips. Stared up at the skies.

And when her gaze fell back upon Eyvind, it was through the eyes of Rib Smasher. Confident. Unshakable. And utterly cold.

"There are two hundred people out there, vulnerable to the mist." She hardened her jaw. "The more of us ready to evacuate them, the better. Tell me which supplies you've gathered, Hakonsson, and I will inform you of our plan."

Eyvind began listing the supplies he'd gathered. With each cart, horse, and weapon he recited, Hekla's heart lightened just a touch. And when he was done, she relayed her plans as promised.

"Let me stand beside you," said Eyvind, snagging her gaze and holding it.

"No," said Hekla. "Istré's locals respect you. They'll trust in your directions far better than mine. And someone must lead them to safety."

A muscle in his jaw flexed, but after a weighted moment, Eyvind nodded.

After agreeing on a signal, Hekla pulled her hood up and turned to retreat down the inn's back road.

"Hekla," said Eyvind. There was weight to her name. As though he wished to say a thousand things. But all he said was, "I'm glad you came back."

Hekla nodded and continued on.

CHAPTER NINETEEN

The sun soon set, but where the moons should have risen was naught but darkness. The double black moon was a rare phenomenon that happened but once a decade, when the sister moons' cycles aligned just right. It felt unnatural not to see at least one of the sisters in the sky, as though the eyes of a great god were shut to this world.

Hekla's legs dangled over the side of the stockade wall, her back propped against a palisade. The forest had been cleared within one hundred paces of the wall, and a sharp, piney scent filled the air. Beyond the wall stretched a graveyard of stumps and felled trees awaiting their turn to become firewood.

Istré's defensive walls were well built. Wooden stakes jutted outward to impale attackers, arrow slits were carved into the timber walls at regular intervals, and watchtowers were stationed at each corner of the town. By all standards, Istré was well fortified. Little good it would do against the mist.

Five of Eyvind's most trusted men were scattered along the stockade wall, five more assembling provisions for the evacuation in the inn's yard. Not long ago, Hekla had spied Gunnar in the town square with a bucket in each hand. Everything was proceeding just as it must, but as low, rhythmic drumbeats began in Istré's town square, Hekla's muscles tensed all the same.

"Tonight, we honor the gods of old!" Loftur bellowed above the drums. "Tonight, we pay penance for seventeen years of neglect!"

Hekla fought the urge to roll her eyes at Loftur's commitment to this ruse.

Enormous wooden platters were brought into the square, bearing portions of a freshly butchered ox. Behind them, warriors rolled the casks of mead reserved for Shortest Day. Eyvind had informed Hekla that each household was ordered to provide their best weapons; tonight, they'd each offer meat, mead, and weapons to Sunnvald.

Hekla braced her elbows on her knees and leaned as far forward as she dared. Over the roofs of Istré's homes, she watched the men and women dressed in their very best. Girls and women wore crowns of autumnal grass, while the men had combed tallow into their hair to set it in place.

Where the hazel staves had once outlined the fighting square, an enormous bonfire now spat sparks into the black skies. Loftur and Konal stood before it, clad in strange-looking robes, and with the men and women of Istré queuing before them. Konal held a small bowl in hand, smudging what appeared to be ashes across the forehead of a woman. The woman drew a weapon from her belt, laying it between her palms while bowing her head to the flames. The blade was then tossed into the bonfire, followed quickly by a cut of oxen and cup of mead.

Hekla watched as the cycle was repeated over and over. It

was a terrible waste of provisions, and she pitied these people for the guilt they would feel when they realized they'd been deceived. The air was soon tinged with the scent of burnt meat, the drumbeats and laughter growing ever louder. Hekla pushed to her feet and turned to survey the dark woods one hundred paces away from Istré.

It was utterly still.

Time dripped by, the feast below only growing more boisterous. Hekla locked eyes with Sigrún in the southernmost watchtower, and the knots in her stomach loosened.

Patience, Sigrún's gaze seemed to urge.

Hekla dipped her head in acknowledgment and glanced at the skies. Without the sister moons, Hekla had trouble judging the time. Surely it was nearing midnight.

A warm breeze ruffed her hair, sending a prickle down Hekla's neck. The acrid scent of burnt meat was heavy and pungent, but there, just beneath it, was the slightest hint of earthen decay. Her spine straightened, and she pushed slowly to her feet. Clutching the sharpened pikes of the wall, Hekla stared into the dark woods, ears straining for any sign of the—

There.

If she hadn't been searching for it, perhaps she'd have missed it. But the low throb vibrated through the timber beams beneath Hekla's feet and sent a shiver straight up her spine. She put her fingers to her lips and let out three sharp whistles.

Her ears strained over the drumbeats and laughter, but she caught the sharp trills in reply, counting until she confirmed all six. Good. Hekla unsheathed the pair of torches strapped to her back. The rough wooden handle felt strange in her hand. She was so used to leather-wrapped hilts, but when it came to the mist, fire was the only protection they had tonight.

Crouching low, she pulled a firestone from her pocket. With a few quick strikes, she had the first torch lit. She touched the second torch to the first and held them high to cast light on the forest surrounding Istré.

Naught but darkness met her eyes.

Yet Hekla could feel the mist's approach like her own heartbeat—could sense its hunger in the marrow of her bones. Tonight, the mortals feasted, and it, too, would gorge. The heartbeat grew stronger though still distant within the woods. Bile rose in her throat as Hekla considered all that was at stake. Should she fail, she and all of Istré would face a fate worse than death.

"Mist!" someone shouted, and Hekla was relieved that at least one of the revelers had enough presence of mind to notice the strange throbbing beneath their feet.

"Hurry!" bellowed Loftur. "All of you come forth and give your offerings! It must all go into the fire!"

Hekla glanced over her shoulder, taking in the scene unfolding. The queue had broken, men and women rushing at the bonfire, tossing weapons in without ceremony. Alf the Slender grabbed the enormous platter of oxen portions, flinging it into the flames. Half the meat splattered onto the packed-earth road, the platter skidding through the fire and colliding with a woman on the opposite side. A pair of young warriors frantically rolled the casks of mead into the blaze.

And above it all, Loftur's frantic shouting: "Accept our offerings, oh mighty mist! Heal our kin as you promised—"

"Mist?" bellowed the armorer. "These offerings are for *Sunnvald*—"

"I have done as you asked, mist beast!" shouted Loftur. "Now you must follow through with your end of the bargain!"

The casks of mead exploded under the bonfire's heat and pressure, and chaos erupted in Istré's square. Accusations of Loftur's betrayal and panicked screams filled the air. Hekla cursed Loftur. Cursed Istré's citizens for not hearing her warning. This could have been avoided if only they'd listened.

Now was not the time for such bitter thoughts. Hekla cast another anxious glance toward the square, and as she caught sight of Eyvind's ridiculous red cloak, she exhaled and turned back to her task.

The first wisps of white seeped from the woods, sending Hekla's pulse skittering. She gripped her torches tighter and counted her breaths. The mist quickly thickened, undulating in time to the distant heartbeat.

Hold, Hekla told herself, fighting against the urge to flee. She could not forget that world of chaos, the sense of the mist permeating her senses . . .

"Mist!" bellowed Loftur with a hint of desperation. "I have done as you asked! I have held your feast, now you must do as you promised!"

Hekla's jaw shifted against her growing pity.

"You must heal my kin!" Loftur's voice broke, and Hekla guessed he was finally realizing that he'd fallen prey to the mist's trickery—that he'd offered the whole of Istré up on a platter.

The villagers screamed in the town center, but Eyvind's voice rang clear above them all. "Citizens of Istré! If you wish to live, you must listen!" The frenzy in the square lessened just a touch. "In the yard behind the Hungry Blade, we have eighteen wagons departing for Kopa. Each of you must follow me with haste. There is enough space for everyone, but if I see any pushing—if anyone so much as raises a fist—my men will restrain you and you will be left behind."

In that moment, Eyvind sounded less like a jarl's son, desperate to win his father's affection, and more like a true leader. Despite the sting of his betrayal, pride shimmered in Hekla's chest. Eyvind had taken a stand for what he knew was right, and because of it, hundreds of lives would be saved.

The voices quickly grew fainter, and Hekla was able to breathe a little easier. Everything was proceeding just as it should.

"What of my kin!" Loftur had fallen to his knees before the raging bonfire. "What of your promise, mist?"

"Come, All-Wise!" shouted Konal. "We've performed the rites. There is nothing else to be done."

"But my *kin,* Konal!"

"You cannot help them if you are dead, Loftur. Gather your wits, and let us get to the wagons."

The mist was now sliding through gaps in the stockade wall. Hekla felt it hesitate. A tendril slid forward, and she drove it back with a slash of her torch. The mist hissed in anger, but she felt the moment it decided she was not worth it.

The mist parted and surged forth, surrounding her on all sides. Heart hammering, Hekla looked up to the small section of star-spattered skies overhead for reassurance. The mist eddied around her and rushed into Istré's streets like a raging river, and she sent a silent prayer that Eyvind's evacuation had been swift and efficient.

Hekla counted her rapid heartbeats to remain calm and hoped Sigrún and Eyvind's men could do the same. Gradually, the mist thinned, and as the last of it churned into the town, Hekla felt as though she could finally breathe.

She shifted the torches to her metal hand, then lifted the trembling fingers of her left to her lips, letting out two sharp whistles.

Hekla leaped down from the wall, knees nearly buckling as they absorbed her weight. Without missing a beat, she broke into a jog, trailing a safe distance behind the mist. Four trills whistled in reply to her signal, then a fifth, but not a sixth. Hekla frowned, worry twisting in her gut.

But she could not allow herself to dwell on it. As the V-shaped pillars marking Istré's town square came into view, Hekla imagined Gunnar touching his torch to the pine resin they'd drizzled along the ground. In her mind's eye, she saw flames bursting skyward, racing along the trail of pitch and creating a fiery barrier between the mist and those wagons.

As if on cue, the mist's rage rattled the air. Had it reached its blistering fence? Found itself trapped?

Hekla jogged down Istré's main road, stopping before the wall of flames. Beyond it, the mist looked like a boiling storm cloud, trapped in a seamless prison of flames as high as a man is tall. She allowed herself this moment of victory, but the mist seemed to sense her presence and turned to her.

With a screech, it surged forward. But as it met the line of fire, the mist jerked back.

Hekla ignored it, pulling out the longbow she'd stashed behind a water barrel. Movement in her periphery signaled Sigrún's arrival.

During their planning session, Sigrún had been steadfast in her assurances that she could complete this part of the task. But as Hekla watched her feet falter—saw the pure, unbridled fear in Sigrún's eyes—doubt crept in. The glossy scarring along Sigrún's neck and scalp glowed orange in the firelight, vanishing under her collar and emerging from the cuff of her left sleeve where it covered the whole of her hand. In all their years together, Sigrún had never spoken of her scars. But her reaction to the flames affirmed Hekla's longheld suspicion—they had been wrought by fire.

"Can you do it?" Hekla asked, inwardly cursing herself. But with her prosthetic hand, Hekla had never been able to grip the bow properly, and Gunnar, well, Rey had once deemed his archery skills to be "worse than a drunken child's."

Sigrún swallowed. Turning, she met Hekla's gaze, eyes hard with determination. Sigrún nodded, taking the bow and quiver of arrows from Hekla.

"We've five minutes or less," growled Gunnar, rushing from the shadows with four of Eyvind's men on his heels. He placed a bucket at Sigrún's feet filled with thick, glossy, and highly flammable pitch.

"The other barrels?" asked Hekla.

"Hidden among the pillars," replied Gunnar.

Her gaze fell upon the V-shaped pillars rising from torrents of flame and smoke. Ten barrels of flammable pine pitch were nestled within the ring of fire where the mist was now trapped. A single well-placed arrow, and the entire square would go up in flames.

"Good," she said.

But Hekla felt the air's sudden shift, the heartbeat growing deeper as though burrowing under the soil. An ominous prickle rushed down her spine. The mist was still trapped within its fiery prison, but she felt certain that something had just happened.

"We might have less than five minutes," said Hekla, left hand finding the hilt of her sword.

Sigrún dipped an arrow into the pitch, then edged cautiously toward the wall of flames to light it. The mist swelled and rippled around the square, testing its confinement with relentless focus. The moment a gap formed in the flames, the mist would sense it.

Sigrún shuffled another inch forward, but it was impossible not to notice the tremble of her hand. The air was thick with smoke and dust, with the pungent char of burnt oxen meat. Hekla threw an elbow over her mouth, in part to stifle the smell, in part to restrain herself from shouting at Sigrún to hurry.

A low, deep growl came from just beyond the stockade walls, and suddenly, Hekla understood what that strange shift had been: The mist had called upon the undead. She held her breath as Sigrún nocked the arrow and aimed it at the dais. The bowstring twanged, the flaming arrow arcing through the air. But Hekla cursed under her breath as she saw it would land just wide of the dais.

The mist rattled in what Hekla perceived as an unsettling laugh, but a snarl from her left had her whirling.

Through the dust and smoke a pair of red eyes glowed. A Turned wolf prowled forward, and Eyvind's men gasped at their first glimpse of it. The beast's coat was matted and torn, its too-wide mouth revealing rows of glinting teeth.

"We guard Sigrún's flank," Hekla barked. "And remember, you must take their heads." As she unsheathed her sword and claws, a grim smile spread across Hekla's lips. With the mist, she was out of her element. But these foes would fall to steel.

Their small group held their ground as a second pair of eyes appeared behind the first, wider and much higher up. An enormous Turned bear ambled out of the mist on elongated limbs that twisted at the wrong angles. Liquid dripped from overlong fangs, while its dagger-sized claws gouged the earthen road.

The third Turned creature to emerge from the smoke was a man, an iron collar banded around his throat. She recognized him at once as the largest of the draugur men chained in the Hagenssons' barn. Hekla did not know if the draugur himself had broken his chains or if the mist had sent another of its Turned creatures to complete the task, but she decided it didn't matter.

"Mortals!" hissed the mist through the draugur's mouth. "Your bright prison will not trap us for long!"

More Turned creatures crept through the smoke—wolves and bears and more freed draugur with chains dragging behind them. Ravens with shredded wings and elongated talons emerged, followed by vampire deer with dagger-sharp antlers, frost foxes with torn and matted fur, forest walkers with three-pronged claws . . .

Hekla's pulse thundered, but her lips formed a smile. "I've always loved a good challenge," she crooned to the mist's avatar, unsheathing her claws. Dropping her voice, she murmured to the warriors around her, "No one gets past us. Our only chance is for Sigrún to set those barrels alight."

They grunted in acknowledgment.

The Turned wolf at the front of the pack leaped forward, and chaos fell upon them.

CHAPTER TWENTY

Planning and leading this impossible task had pushed Hekla beyond her comfort, but as her world descended into mayhem, her uncertainty dissolved in an instant. With Turned creatures prowling into Istré, Hekla lost herself to instinct, becoming a creature of cold steel and ruthless violence. In battle, there was no time for thinking, no time for emotion. There was only the need to spill the putrid black blood of these Turned creatures.

There was also the unmistakable thrum of pride in her veins. Adept at delivering death, Hekla had come so very far from the helpless woman she'd once been. On the battlefield, she was in her element, doing what she was born to do.

Hekla supposed she ought to thank Rothna for helping her discover her calling in life. Her former husband had, after all, taught Hekla her first lessons in brutality. But her brutality was not the same as his. She didn't fight to feel bigger, more powerful. She fought for those who could not. For the girl she'd once been.

A lethal longsword in her left hand was the weapon her enemies saw coming. But the five curving steel claws on her right were their undoing. She dazzled her enemies with showy arcs of her longsword, while delivering death in vicious slashes of her prosthetic's claws. It was poetic, Hekla supposed—she'd molded what one might consider a weakness into her greatest weapon.

In the midst of battle, Hekla relied less on her head and more on her heart—on that knowing feeling deep in her chest—to keep her from danger. She danced away from fangs a handspan long, ducked beneath hacking claws and snarling maws, and slashed through the neck of a wolf lunging at Gunnar. All the while, Hekla listened through the din of battle for Sigrún's shrill whistle, which would signify success. But as her world became a storm of violence, time grew shifty.

From the edge of her vision, Hekla noted several Turned beasts slinking away. While raking her claws through a Turned bear's flank, she shifted to investigate. And as a grimwolf lay itself down upon the flaming barrier, a scream tore from her throat.

"No!"

Hekla turned on her foot, charging toward the wolf. Immediately, the flames stuttered, creating a gap in the wall. But as the wolf's fur caught flame, it was enough to bar the mist from slinking through. Hekla fell upon the wolf, heaving it off the fire by its tail, before decapitating the beast with a brutal hack of her blade.

Fire flickered back across the smear of flammable resin on the soil where the grimwolf had just lain. But there was no time for her to pause. Horror coursed through her as she caught sight of a human draugur now laying herself down on the flames. As her screams reached an ear-piercing pitch, Hekla lunged at her next. By the time she'd put the wretched woman out of her misery, a vampire deer had laid itself down farther along the line.

The mist lurched toward the creature, undulating as the flames covering the vampire deer's fur began to sputter. Hekla grabbed its leg, heaving with all her effort, but the deer moved scarcely an inch. Farther along the ring of fire, other creatures were laying themselves down, smothering the flames.

Helplessness twisted her insides, but Hekla did not relent, using the full force of her body weight to heave the deer another inch.

"You see, sly mortal?" gloated the mist through a nearby human draugur. "You cannot best us."

With her heart palpitating wildly, the peace Hekla had felt earlier was now nowhere to be found. She couldn't move this enormous deer in time, let alone reach the other creatures laying themselves down. Soon, a gap would form in the fire wall, and their chance to end the mist would be gone. If only Sigrún could set those barrels alight before then . . . but a glance over her shoulder had Hekla's stomach wrenching. Perched atop a rain barrel, Sigrún had spun away from her task, firing arrow after arrow at the Turned creatures; they'd broken past Gunnar and the other warriors and were now closing in on her.

Hekla turned to face the mist head-on. Perhaps this was it—the moment death finally claimed her. If so, she would go with steel in her hand and the knowledge that she'd done all she could to keep the people of Istré safe. By now, they'd be miles down the road on their way to Kopa. Hekla held out hope that it was too far for the mist to travel, even on this, of all nights.

"Hekla!" The shout came from behind her, but she could not look away from her task. With a roar, Hekla yanked with the full force of her weight, budging the vampire deer another paltry inch.

"We have tasted your strength," growled the mist through a draugur, "and we want you in our ranks. We will snap your threads and forge them to our will."

Nausea churned inside Hekla at the thought. The flames covering the vampire deer's corpse were all but sputtered out. A tendril of mist slid along its singed coat, probing, seeking, sliding . . .

Suddenly the tiny, faltering flame erupted violently, so high and brutally hot, it sent Hekla sprawling backward.

"Ashbringer," the mist's avatar growled.

Hekla watched in stunned disbelief as warriors charged forth, colliding with the Turned monsters. It took her a moment to understand that it was the rest of Eyvind's retinue—the warriors who ought to be evacuating Istré's citizens.

Suddenly Eyvind himself was beside her, his men charging behind her and joining the battle with sword and shield. Hekla would have bellowed her joy at his timely arrival, but the sight of him rendered her speechless. Eyvind's hazel eyes reflected the blaze before them.

And from his palms streamed jets of flames, filling all the gaps in the mist's fiery prison.

CHAPTER TWENTY-ONE

Hekla's gaze bounced from the flames pouring from Eyvind's palms to the gaps in the fire wall, now blocked. "Hakonsson," she sputtered. "You're—how are you—"

She was unable to finish the sentence. Eyvind Bloody Hakonsson was one of the Galdra. Hekla had never seen magic wielded before, and for a moment, all she could do was stare in wonder. Was this how Eyvind and Rey knew each other? Was there some sort of secret Galdra club?

Hekla's mind reeled, but there was no time for her to put things together. Help had come when they needed it most, and she would take it in any form. A Turned grimwolf lunged at Eyvind's back, and Hekla buried her claws in its throat, wrenching downward to bring it crashing to the ground. She twisted and drove her longsword down hard, severing the beast's head.

"Kill the Ashbringer!" howled a draugur in the mist's inhuman voice.

Hekla felt the creatures' focus shift toward Eyvind, and her anger burned awake, low and deep inside her.

"Not on my watch." Hekla hefted her sword and placed her back to Eyvind's. The heat pouring off him made the air hotter than a steam bath, and sweat beaded her brow, sliding down her temple.

"So protective, Lynx," said Eyvind, a smile in his voice.

"Save your strength, Fox!" she barked, fighting the urge to roll her eyes, because of course this man would tease her while they were but a heartbeat from death's door.

As a Turned bear lunged forward, Hekla braced for impact. She had to protect Eyvind. Could not allow the undead beasts to break his focus.

"The dais, Eyvind. Can you set the dais aflame?"

But Eyvind just grunted, and as Hekla turned her head slightly, she saw two fresh gaps form in the wall as more creatures laid themselves down. Twin jets of flame burst from Eyvind's palms as he quickly filled the newly formed gaps. It seemed he required all of his strength and concentration to contain the mist within Istré's square, which meant Sigrún needed to set that gods-damned dais alight, and she needed to do it *now*.

Hekla could not risk checking on Sigrún's progress; the surge of Turned creatures seemed endless, each one Hekla felled replaced by two more. She buried her sword in a vampire deer's neck. With a quick kick to the beast's chest, she heaved her sword loose and hacked until its head fell free. From the corner of her eye, she saw that Eyvind's men had cordoned a large group of Turned against a longhouse, but a male scream from that direction suggested their ranks had now broken.

At last, there was a break in the onslaught. Sigrún had an arrow nocked in her bow and aimed toward the dais, but a grimwolf snapped at her ankles. She lurched back, toppling off the rain barrel. As the grimwolf leaped onto her, Hekla opened her mouth to cry out but shut it as Gunnar vaulted through the air and fell upon the beast.

On Hekla's left, a forest walker advanced, and she was momentarily stunned. With rough, bark-like skin and branch-like arms, the forest walker's three-pronged claws lashed out with inhuman speed. Hekla ducked with scarcely a heartbeat to spare.

"The dais!" she shouted to Eyvind. "Burn the dais!" Hekla kicked out low, her boot colliding with solid wood. The forest walker did not so much as budge. How could she take its head?

The forest walker swung again, and this time, Hekla was a heartbeat too slow. Pain exploded from her shoulder, sending her staggering back. The beast surged after her. A scream tore from her throat as its claw shredded through her breeches and into the flesh of her upper thighs.

"Hekla!" bellowed Eyvind, but his voice sounded distant through the loud ring in her ears. Her knees buckled as the forest walker advanced. Though its eyes were a vacant red haze, she could have sworn she read victory in them. Thick, gnarled arms swung upward, and for the dozenth time that hour, Hekla prepared to meet death.

A dull *thwack* met Hekla's ears, confusion jostling through her as the forest walker's smile fell. Black blood oozed like sticky sap, dripping down its trunk. A gleaming axe sang through the air and embedded deep in the forest walker's neck. The beast whirled, but it was too late. A third swing of the axe knocked the forest walker's head clean off. Putrid black blood spurted from its headless trunk, but it was the most beautiful sight Hekla had ever seen. She met Thrand's blue eyes. The warrior's once-gleaming armor was now smeared with ash and gore. As he yanked her to her feet, she smiled.

"Finally put some scuffs in that armor, Long Sword?"

"Aye."

"Is she hurt?" grunted Eyvind.

"Merely a flesh wound," Hekla assured him, but she frowned. With a wide stance, he seemed to brace against the power churning from his palms. His limbs trembled with exertion, and rivulets of sweat carved paths through his soot-stained face. It was clear Eyvind could not continue like this for long.

More of the Turned charged at Eyvind, and Hekla and Thrand worked in tandem to cut them down. Turned after Turned fell, but more surged forth. The attacks grew more frenzied, their parries more sluggish, and Hekla was alarmed to find her battle thrill waning.

They could not keep on like this. Eyvind now blocked more gaps in the fire than she could count, and chaos engulfed Sigrún's corner of the square. The moment the mist escaped its fiery confines, they would all be consumed and Turned. They needed to change the tide of battle—needed to try something else.

"You see, mortal?" cackled the mist through a nearby draugur. "It is inevitable. It is fated. We will finish what we started. You *will* belong to us."

Hekla slashed into a grimwolf's throat, refusing to let the

mist distract her. Pungent black blood slid down her claws and coated her metal arm. But the mist's taunting words stirred an idea. It was brash. It was almost certainly mad.

But no one had ever called her levelheaded.

"Cover Hakonsson's back," she grunted to Thrand, driving her sword into a grimwolf. "Let me into the ring," she shouted to Eyvind. "The moment the mist's attention is diverted, order a retreat. And once they're gone, Eyvind, you must push the full force of your magic onto the dais."

"Hekla, no—"

"There are ten casks of pitch ready to vaporize this gods-damned mist. The moment the dais catches, you turn and flee, Eyvind. Promise me that."

"No," grunted Eyvind. "You'll die."

A sudden wave of tenderness crashed through her, and Hekla couldn't help but smile. "Don't worry for me, Foxie. The lynx, after all, is a cat." She edged around him, ducking under the inferno surging from his palms. "Which means we have nine lives."

"Don't you—"

"I'm jumping into that ring whether you pause your fire or not, Hakonsson. I'd prefer not to char before facing the mist, but it is your choice!"

Angry, desperate words spewed from Eyvind. "You maddening, stubborn, irrational woman—"

She cut him off with a warm, firm kiss. Hekla didn't care that his men might see her. Didn't care what they might think. For a fraction of a heartbeat, she was back on that riverbank, opening herself to a man for the first time in years.

And in this kiss, she let him see it all—the girl she'd once been, the one who still lived deep inside this toughened warrior. The one who'd come out, if only for a night.

Hekla had to force herself to pull back. "Thank you," she whispered for only Eyvind to hear, "for reminding me of who I am." She allowed herself to stare into those hazel eyes, now wild with anger, with fear, with utter despair.

And then she was turning to the wall of flames, time slowing as she drew a deep breath. And before doubt could creep in, Hekla hurled herself into the inferno. Without a heartbeat to spare, Eyvind's fire extinguished, a gap forming in the wall of flames. She landed on the balls of her feet and glanced over her shoulder. An incredulous laugh fell from her lips. Eyvind had reignited his fiery jets, encasing her within the mist's blazing prison.

Hekla rose to her feet and turned to face the churning, undulating mass of white.

She smiled. Blew it a kiss. "Hello, dúlla. You want me? Well, here I am."

The air rattled with the mist's anger, the smoke and pungent reek of charred corpses choking her lungs. Beyond the wall of flames, there was some sort of commotion, but Hekla did not dare take her eyes off the mist.

"You meddlesome mortal!" raged the mist through its draugur. "We will consume you!"

"Mmm hmm. You said that already."

The mist turned into a storm of anger, causing Hekla to retreat a step. Yet she felt its attention upon her and hoped it was enough of a diversion to allow Eyvind to set those barrels alight. The blistering heat of the wall of flames at her back blocked her further retreat. The mist undulated with glee, advancing upon her.

This was it.

“Down!” came the cry, not a moment before a solid mass crashed into Hekla.

Darkness engulfed her.

And the world erupted.

CHAPTER TWENTY-TWO

The thunder was no slow rolling wave building in increments, but destruction striking upon her with sudden force. The ground shook with its impact, the air scorching like the heat of a thousand suns. It was blistering agony so hot that Hekla thought she'd melt.

Beyond the darkness came a scream of anguish. The mist's heavy presence in the air fragmented, lessening with each passing second . . .

Hekla screamed, too, sizzling as though she bathed in the thick orange lifeblood of a fire mountain. Writhing, she pleaded with the gods to grant her the mercy of death. The air she gasped in seared her lungs, while the blood in her veins boiled. Each torturous heartbeat bled into the next, making Hekla want to claw out of her skin. But then the heat abated, just a touch, then a little less. And then it rolled right over her, leaving her gasping in darkness.

Was she dead? Was this the darkness of a night sky? Would she follow the Mother Star to her final resting place among her ancestors?

But then something moved above her. *Someone* moved.

And suddenly, Hekla understood what the smothering darkness was, or, she should say, *who* it was. Eyvind gods-damned Hakonsson had thrown himself over her. Had somehow kept her from roasting to a crisp.

"Eyvind?" she gasped, rolling him gently off her and onto his back.

His low groan had her exhaling in relief. He was alive, thank the gods above. But how? Fires raged all around them—on the dais, the pillars, the turfed roofs surrounding the square. Hekla's gaze roamed over him as she tried to understand. His hair was singed, and there were patches of burnt skin on his beautiful face, but the red cloak she hated so much was perfectly untouched.

"You fool of a man," she choked out, even as her hands smoothed a singed lock of hair from his face. "You've burnt your pretty hair." To her horror, tears gathered in her eyes.

Eyvind's expression morphed into concern. "It will grow back."

"You won't be able to braid it!"

His hand stroked reassuringly along her left arm. "Then I shan't."

"But it is all different lengths! You'll look a fool." Hekla burned with embarrassment as she swiped a tear from her cheek.

Eyvind was losing the battle against a smile. "Then I'll shave it all off. Perhaps I'll adorn my skull with tattoos. What say you to another dragon?"

Hekla's scowl could shatter stone. "You gods-damned golden boy, you simply had to go and risk your life like that!"

"Aye, but I did."

She smacked his chest with her left hand. "No, you didn't!"

Eyvind captured her wrist and yanked her down onto

him. They were so near their noses nearly touched. "Yes," whispered Eyvind, "I did."

Hekla was beyond thinking—beyond reason and logic. Instinct took hold and she lowered her lips to his. Reveled in the way they fit together so perfectly. Their survival felt like one of Silla's signs from the gods. This kiss was predestined. Fated. Championed by the highest powers of Íseldur.

Flames raged all around them, the entire village now alight. But the smoke and lingering rot of the Turned beasts faded away, as did the pain radiating from Hekla's injuries. Nothing mattered in this moment, because Eyvind was kissing her back—was telling her with his lips all the ways he cared for her. How much he'd feared for her. How glad he was that she'd survived. And in return, she told him how sorry she was for being so stubborn. How she wished she'd trusted in him from the start. How she'd work on being more open.

This kiss was nothing like the ones they'd shared before. Then, they'd been the Fox and the Lynx. But here, amid the flaming ruins of Istré, their lips met as Hekla and Eyvind, and there was something altogether different about that. Hekla's body felt as hot as the fires raging around them, and gods, but she wanted this man, right here, right now.

His grip on her hip turned rough and demanding, a low rumbling sound coming from deep in his chest, and Hekla was glad to find she was not alone in this. Not the only one feeling reckless and needy.

Eyvind drew back, just long enough to mutter, "Gods, I've wanted to—"

But he didn't finish the thought. His hand was in her hair, hauling Hekla's mouth back down to his. She was melting against him, burning like the town all around them, ready to give herself to him right here and now.

A loud crack split the air, and they broke apart.

"The Hungry Blade," said Eyvind, his gaze fixed on something over her shoulder. "It shall soon collapse."

Propped on her left elbow, Hekla's chest heaved as she looked down at him, her insides shimmering with desire and need. But the collapse of the beam was the reminder she needed. They were in the midst of an inferno and had to get out of here.

"Later," she muttered in promise to Eyvind—to herself—not bothering to clarify what she meant by the statement.

Slowly, Hekla sat up, their reality coming into stark focus. Istré was a bonfire, the whole town alight. Horror and sorrow battled within Hekla as she wondered how it had come to this. Carcasses of Turned beasts littered the road, some smoldering like the homes around them. But her gaze snagged on Eyvind's cloak, still a pristine, brilliant red. Hekla frowned.

Following her gaze, Eyvind lifted the hem of his red cloak, unscathed by the blast that had decimated the square. "Fireproof," he said proudly. "A safety precaution for Galdra Ashbringers."

Her gaze shot to his. "Is this how you know Axe Eyes?"

Eyvind pushed to his feet and offered Hekla a hand up. "Aye," he said. "Rey fostered with us one summer, and the rest is history. A good, solid warrior to call friend." He slid an arm around Hekla's shoulder and steered her toward Istré's main thoroughfare.

"Eyvind," said Hekla, stepping around a Turned grimwolf corpse, "your father."

The arm around her shoulder stiffened, and Eyvind let out a long exhale. "Someone once told me that sometimes those we love most are undeserving."

"That *someone* sounds wise."

From the corner of her eye, she caught the quirk of his lips. "On some occasions, perhaps. On others, a mulish, self-sacrificing fool."

Hekla harrumphed. But she rested her head on his shoulder and whispered, "You did the right thing. Your choice saved many lives tonight."

It might have been her imagination, but the tension in Eyvind's muscles seemed to ease just a touch.

"*We* saved many lives," he corrected.

Hekla huffed. "I suppose that makes us both self-sacrificing fools."

Eyvind squeezed her shoulders. "I suppose it does."

CHAPTER TWENTY-THREE

Hekla's limbs felt heavy as she took in the extent of Istré's devastation. The heat was near unbearable where the homes were close together, fire leaping from roof to roof, eating its way down the timber walls. As the Hungry Blade, reduced to a skeleton of beams, collapsed in a heap, it was clear that come morning, no structure would be left standing.

They'd defeated the mist—for now—and had evacuated Istré's people before harm could befall them. And yet, Hekla felt like a failure. She'd come to help these people, not burn their village to the ground. And she couldn't help but wonder if a better leader would have succeeded where she'd failed.

At last, they ducked beneath Istré's burning gates and stepped onto the Black Road. Turning, Hekla took in the inferno that once had been Istré. Thankfully, the wide, barren plains encircling the town provided a barrier between Istré and the surrounding woods, and as she caught sight of warriors stamping out small fires along this perimeter, she said a silent prayer that they could keep it contained.

As Hekla and Eyvind approached, a small gathering of warriors erupted in whoops and cheers. Hekla spotted Gunnar and Sigrún among them, and a wide grin split her cheeks. She broke into a hobbled run to greet them.

Thank the gods, signed Sigrún, and she nearly tackled Hekla to the ground in a hug. But beneath her fierce grip, Sigrún shook, and after releasing Hekla, she brushed tears from her cheeks.

I'm sorry, she signed. *I thought I could*—But Sigrún's hands trembled too hard for her to finish.

Hekla placed her metal hand on Sigrún's shoulder. "Do not be sorry," Hekla said, signing in tandem. "The mist is gone, its creatures dead. It's over for now."

She tried to ignore the worry wriggling at those last two words. *For now.* Because, much like the mist that had dissipated under moonlight, more could be formed from wherever it originated deep in the woods. No. This job wasn't over. She sensed it had barely started.

But for now, Hekla's grin broadened as Gunnar gathered her in a rib-bruising hug.

"Too many times," he said into her hair, squeezing ever tighter. "No more throwing yourself into death's path. No more endangering yourself."

Hekla pushed on his chest, wincing as the wound at her shoulder pulled. "Easy, Fire Fist. I cannot breathe."

Reluctantly, Gunnar released her, looking sheepish as Hekla rubbed her tender shoulder. "No more endangering myself? Gods above, Gunnar, I'm no milk maiden. What's gotten into you?"

Gunnar's dark eyes held a strange, unreadable look. "It's only that—I cannot—I wish to speak to you of something—"

His gaze drifted to something over her shoulder. "Later. We shall speak of it later."

And then Gunnar launched himself at a startled Eyvind, wrapping him in a bear hug. "You saved her, Hakonsson," Gunnar blubbered.

"You needn't thank me, warrior, truly—"

"Aye, but I must!" Gunnar rocked Eyvind back and forth, and Hekla couldn't help but snicker.

Hours later, Hekla sighed in contentment. She soaked in a large wooden tub, steam rising from the water and carrying the scent of calendula. The wounds at her shoulder and thigh had been cleaned, her belly filled with stew and bread. This bath was the last step before she collapsed onto her bed in complete exhaustion.

It had been nearly first light by the time the last of the fires around Istré had been stamped out and their group took to the road. They'd reached the nearest village at midday, and immediately, Eyvind had shifted into the leader's role. For once, Hekla was glad to let him. In an imperious move that was true to the son of a jarl, he bought out the entire inn, and had the innkeeper and his servants scurrying about within moments of their arrival. Their horses were led away to the stables out back, while washing basins were fetched so the crew could wipe the ash from their faces. The village healer had been called for, and a cauldron of stew soon simmered over the cookfire.

Now she lounged blissfully in the tub, her metal arm lying

on the floor next to it. Slowly, heat melted into her weary bones, the calendula soothing her aches. The warm water wicked dirt and ash from her body, while the herbal blend relaxed her.

The thrill of surviving that blast had long faded from her body, yet Hekla was startled to find her tender feelings for Eyvind had lingered. She could still feel the imprint of his lips against hers—could still feel the impact of what he'd done.

Yes, he'd hidden things from her, and she could not forget the humiliation of being cast off the job in front of his retinue. And yet, in the light of day, she now saw things differently. When he'd discovered her on that road, barefoot and clad only in a tunic, Eyvind hadn't known she'd been abducted by a squirrel and taken to the Hagensson farm. When she put herself in Eyvind's boots, Hekla could see how disrespectful her actions had looked.

Despite her deranged actions, Eyvind had still listened to her. And bigger than that, he'd gone against his father's orders, double-crossing both Konal and Loftur. The realization that he'd been listening to her all this time filled Hekla with gratitude that was impossible to put into words. He'd trusted her. Had respected her. And she . . . she'd defied him at every turn. Threatened to gut him. Had forced him into a corner, where the only choice had been to throw her from the job.

Hekla groaned, dipping her head beneath the water.

As she broke the surface, she was filled with the sudden need to see Eyvind. Something had profoundly shifted between them in Istré's town square, and she wanted to be certain he'd felt it, too. All sorts of new truths were bubbling up inside her—that she liked how she felt when she was with him, and that if he was willing, perhaps this could be a fresh start.

Perhaps they could be a *them*.

In a dreamlike state, Hekla pulled herself from the tub, dried herself off, then dressed in her clean clothes—clothes that were thankfully undamaged as they'd been safely stored in her gelding's saddlesacks. She ran a comb through her hair, smiling like a wolverine.

But a boisterous knock at the door diverted her attention. Before Hekla could open it, Gunnar strode in.

"Fire Fist—" she started, breaking off as she took in his appearance. He was clad in his finest doublet, and his white teeth flashed from a broad smile. His locs and beard were adorned with silver cuffs and gleamed as though freshly oiled. Hekla thought back to the state he'd been in just a few weeks before and was amazed at how far the warrior had come.

"You're well attired" was all she could manage.

Ever the showman, Gunnar lifted his arms, spinning in a slow circle for Hekla to get the full effect.

Hekla put her hands on her hips. "What has you looking so handsome?"

That broad, confident smile deepened as Gunnar strolled forward. He worked a hemp sack loose from his belt.

"For you," he said, bowing low and placing the bag in Hekla's hand with a flourish.

It was surprisingly heavy, filled with sólas and kressens. "What is this?"

"'Tis your bride price."

Hekla stared, dumbstruck, trying to understand this new jest. Gunnar's thick black brows lifted in expectation, and she scrambled for a reply, but words seemed to have fled her in this moment.

He chuckled, completely unfazed by her vacant expression. "Ahh, but you want me to do this the traditional way?" He drew his sword, then dropped to his knees, laying the flat of the blade across his palms. Bowing his head, Gunnar recited, "Fairest maiden, I pledge to you my sword, my heart, my love—"

"Gunnar."

His brow lifted, and he sent her a scathing look. "Let me finish. Where was I? My love. I vow to shelter you, to provide for you, to lie with no other woman. I kneel before you now to ask for your hand."

Apparently now finished, Gunnar lifted his head and beamed at her.

Acid burned in her stomach and climbed up her throat. What in the eternal fucking fires had gotten into him?

But at her silence, Gunnar's head cocked to the side. "Ah, I see. You truly wish to be wooed, do you?"

Placing the sword down on the floor, he mocked rolling up his sleeves, then took her hand in his. "The past two months have shown me a long life is far from guaranteed. I've travelled far and wide within this realm. Have tasted adventure and earned my share of scars. Now I am ready to rest my feet, to build a home and a family. And I would do it with you by my side, Hekla Rib Smasher—" He paused, apparently in search of her family name.

Hekla's mouth opened and closed, still unable to speak.

"That is only part of your bride price," Gunnar continued.

"I've more buried in my hoard near Kopa. Should you need proof, I shall dig it up and show you once we're near."

Hekla pulled her hand free from his to rub her throbbing temples, and Gunnar's smile fell just a fraction. And in that moment, she knew—this was no jest. This fool of a man was truly asking for her hand.

He cleared his throat. "I know you've no love for your brother, and I would not do you the dishonor of asking him for your hand. Instead, I ask *you,* Hekla Rib Smasher—"

The throbbing in her skull grew ever louder. This had to stop. Hekla tugged at his elbow. "Get up, you brute!"

Gunnar scrambled to his feet. She looked up at the lout, mind scrambling for a way out of this.

"You know I shall never marry again." Hekla tried to keep the desperation from her voice, but a note cracked in.

"We need not have a ceremony." Gunnar's broad shoulders lifted and fell. "But think of the little warriors we could make together. A whole brood of them."

"Brood," she choked out. Her throat was constricting. She could not breathe. Hekla's mind careened like an out-of-control wagon. This was Gunnar, a man she'd used to scratch an itch whenever it arose. She'd been direct with him from the start: only sex and no soft sentiments. Never mind that she hadn't craved his company in weeks.

Yet even through her growing panic, Hekla knew she cared for Gunnar, though if she had to name it, perhaps it was more like the love for a brother. How could she *not* care for him when she'd fought shoulder-to-shoulder with Gunnar for five long years—when they'd weathered so much in the recent seasons? And she could not forget that Gunnar had only just pulled himself out of his misery. She could not risk sending him back there.

Hekla forced a smile on her face. Patted Gunnar's cheek. She watched the confidence in his gaze swirl with confusion.

"I am honored by your request," she managed through her nausea. "I am not saying *no*. I am only saying I need time to think." *Of how to say no while ensuring you won't fall back into a pit of despair,* she could not add.

And before she could witness any hint of hurt on Gunnar's face, Hekla rushed out of the room.

CHAPTER TWENTY-FOUR

Hekla's mind was a jumbled mess, but her feet moved sensibly through the corridor in search of Eyvind's quarters. She was exhausted, yet her body tingled with the need to get away from her lodgings—away from Gunnar kneeling before her . . .

I kneel before you now to ask for your hand.

A hot, restless feeling climbed through her. Hekla *needed* to see Eyvind—needed to see his too-pretty face and hear his arrogant voice. Perhaps he would let her tend to his singed hair or wash the soot from his face. Perhaps she would spend the night in his quarters.

A frisson rushed through her at the very thought. Rather than a twinge of worry, the thought was accompanied by a burst of excitement.

As she neared the innkeeper's quarters—the largest, he'd repeatedly assured Eyvind, before handing him the keys—voices drifted into the corridor, making Hekla's heart quicken.

"Your father will be furious." This voice belonged to Thrand Long Sword, and Hekla was curiously glad to hear it.

"I do not care what he thinks," said Eyvind sharply. "I own

my choice. The people of Istré survived, no thanks to Konal and his rites."

"Your choice affects more than just yourself," grumbled Thrand.

Eyvind was silent a moment before he replied. "I know it affects you and the rest of the lads as well. But Thrand, you know in your heart it was the right thing to do."

"Aye, but it was," muttered Thrand, clearly exasperated. "But I speak not only of your father's orders." There was a note in his voice that made Hekla's feet falter.

"Speak plainly," said Eyvind, the exhaustion in his voice easily heard.

"Don't think I've forgotten that kiss Rib Smasher planted on you," said Thrand. When Eyvind didn't reply, he continued, "And there's the way your eyes follow her constantly—"

"Leave it be, Thrand," warned Eyvind.

But Thrand was not so easily dissuaded. "Had you asked me a week ago, I'd have thought you were madder than a berserker to go anywhere near that woman. But now . . ." Thrand grew silent a moment. "Now, I *suppose* I can see it."

A grunt told Hekla that Eyvind had likely punched his second in command.

"Arse," muttered Thrand. "Have you told her the whole truth? Does she know of Liv?"

Hekla's skin prickled in warning. Who in the eternal fucking fires was *Liv*?

"It was supposed to be a one-night thing," said Eyvind defensively. "I thought—" He sighed, apparently unable to complete the thought.

Thrand let out a dramatic exhale. "Eyvie. It is clear there's no leaving this one behind. I don't know what it is between you, but this job with the mist is far from over. You owe her the truth about your betrothal."

The ground seemed to fall out from beneath Hekla's feet.

Betrothal.

Eyvind gods-damned Hakonsson was betrothed?

An ache bloomed in her chest, pumping through her veins with each beat of her heart. The soft, newly exposed part of her shriveled in despair. Wrong. How could she have been so wrong? How could she have broken her rules and been willing to set them aside for this man?

The pain of this deception sent her back in time—back to a barn where Rothna had loomed over her with that axe in his hand. Hadn't she vowed in that instant never again to trust a man with the softest parts of her? Hadn't she vowed to build up her defenses so high and so strong that no one would ever be able to hurt her again?

The part of her left vulnerable in the wake of the blast now burrowed back down deep inside. Hekla built up her walls. Pulled her warrior's mask into place. She wanted to scream. Wanted to stride into that room and punch Eyvind Hakonsson in his beautiful mouth. Instead, she turned on her heel and strode away from his quarters.

Somehow, Hekla made it outdoors. The air in the yard was crisp with the late-autumn chill, the sun now descending from its zenith as the stablehands readied the horses for the next hard leg of the journey. She rushed behind the barn, then bent double, trying to control her nausea.

Betrothed. All this time, Eyvind had been betrothed. To think of the things she'd shared with him . . . and to think that after that explosion in Istré, she'd been open to the idea of a *them*.

It's better to bruise now, she told herself, *than to break later.*

Swamped by her emotion, Hekla failed to see the small creature bounding along the fence until it was directly beside her. With a gasp, she whirled to face the squirrel.

Kritka looked very far to find you, came the childlike voice in her head. *If we weren't bound to you, Kritka might have lost your scent.*

"No," mumbled Hekla, stumbling back.

Protector must return to the woods. Our mistress is waiting.

"For the last time," she said in a low voice, glancing around to ensure the stablehands could not hear her, "I am not your Protector."

The squirrel reared up, releasing an angry chittering torrent. *Kritka helped you, Protector. Kritka brought you gifts. Helped you seek answers about the dark thing. Now Protector must help our mistress.*

She ran a frazzled hand over her hair. "I must return to Kopa. Seek help from others—"

But the squirrel's head cocked to the side, and coldness began to gather in Hekla's gut. *Long has our mistress been calling for help. Did Protector not find the symbols?*

Hekla's knees felt weak, the cold pit in her stomach widening. "Symbols?" she repeated numbly, but then she understood. The dead Klaernar strung by vines to the pillars. The Spiral Staves etched in blood all around them. The grove with that tree, Spiral Stave twisted into its bark . . .

"That was your mistress," she said numbly.

The squirrel chittered in agreement. *Mistress sent her*

wolves out to all corners of Íseldur to seek out the Protector. Kritka found the scent and then lost it. But then we found you once more . . . You must help Kritka's mistress. Only the Protector can defeat the dark thing.

"The dark thing," repeated Hekla slowly. The mist?

The dark thing grows stronger, Protector. Now it can escape the woods. Soon it will venture even farther.

Thoughts swirled inside Hekla's skull. "And your mistress," she asked the squirrel, "she can help defeat the mist?"

The squirrel tilted its head to the side and regarded her. *Mistress is very wise—knows many things. Kritka knows only to fetch the Protector to free her.*

Hekla folded her arms over her chest, regarding the small creature before her. For so long, she'd rejected the notion that this squirrel could be more than a fever dream. But in the past weeks, she had seen things beyond her wildest imaginings. Was it truly such a stretch to think that there could be more?

And Hekla knew one thing for certain—if they were to defeat the murderous mist, they needed every weapon they could get their hands on.

"Very well, Kritka," said Hekla, voice resolute.

The squirrel's ears perked up, his tail twitching in excitement.

"I will do it. I will free your mistress. But first, I must go to Kopa. We need reinforcements. And we must warn the others of the true dangers of this foe."

With that, she turned her back on the squirrel, glad for a diversion from all that had transpired in the past hour. Hekla needed to fetch her bags. Needed to get away from this place—from Gunnar, who'd asked for her hand, and from Eyvind, who'd bruised her heart.

She needed to get to Kopa. Regroup and gather reinforcements.

And then, she would meet the mist in its own territory. This time, there would be no man to bar her—no rules for her to abide.

Hekla would defeat this mist, or it would defeat her.

THE END [for now]

Pronunciation Guide

Many of the words and names in this book are derived from Old Norse and/or Icelandic; *ð* and *þ* characters have been converted to *th* and *æ* to *ae* for readability

Bjáni—byan-ee
Dúlla—doo-la
Eystri—ay-stree
Flíta—flee-ta
Hevrít—hev-reet
Hjarta—h-yar-ta
Hver—kveh-r
Hvíta—kvee-ta
Íseldur—ees-el-door
Klaernar—klite-nar
Kunta—koon-ta
Lébrynja—lyeh-bryn-ya
Myrkur—mihr-koor
Nordur—nor-door
Reykfjord—rake-fyoord
Róa—roh-a
Signe—sig-nuh
Skjöld—shkuld

Skógungar—shkoon-gar
Slátrari—slow-trar-ee
Stjarna—styat-na
Sudur—soo-door
Urka—oor-ka
Vestir—vest-eer

Glossary

Berskium – a powder mined near Reykfjord; taken by the Klaernar to maintain their large stature and strength

Bjáni – fool (an insult)

Brennsa – fire whiskey

Dúlla – doll (a term of endearment among women)

Eisa Volsik – former princess of Íseldur who was murdered by King Ivar, her body impaled upon a pillar in the pits of Askaborg Castle

Eystri – the easternmost territory of Íseldur

Flíta – phoenix-like butterflies whose wings light up when they fly; in their old age, they burst into flames, and a caterpillar emerges from the ashes

Galdra – a magic-wielding person, also called Ashen; outlawed by King Ivar

Galdur – magic itself

Gothi – a priest of the Ursinian religion

Hábrók – the god of battle, honor, luck, and weather; one of the old gods of Íseldur

Hevrít – an Íseldurian long-bladed dagger

Hindrium – a specialized metal that inhibits the magical abilities of the Galdra

Hóra – whore

Illmarr – a scaled vampire of the sea; it can be lured by eel blood and felled by rowan arrows

Íseldur – kingdom of Ice and Fire; the island nation where this book takes place

Ivar Ironheart – the new king of Íseldur who seized the throne from King Kjartan Volsik seventeen years ago

Kalasgarde – a town in the north of Íseldur, located in Nordur lands

Karthia – an isle to the south of Íseldur

Kjartan Volsik – former king of Íseldur; murdered by King Ivar using the blood-eagle method in the pits of Askaborg Castle

Klaernar – King Ivar's specialized soldiers, also known as the King's Claws

Kopa – a large stone city in the northern parts of Eystri territory

Kunta – cunt (an insult)

Lébrynja – specialized, lightweight armor made of tiny leather-like scales and worn by the Bloodaxe Crew

Malla – the goddess of love, war, and death; one of the old gods of Íseldur; also, the name of one of the moons

Marra – the goddess of knowledge, healing, and peace; one of the old gods of Íseldur; also, the name of one of the moons

Medovukha – a Zagadkian alcoholic beverage similar to mead and made from fermented honey

Myrkur – the god of chaos and darkness; one of the old gods of Íseldur

Nordur – the northernmost territory of Íseldur

Norvaland – the isle northeast of Íseldur; it was overthrown by Ivar's father, Harald, who now sits on the throne

Róa – a hot beverage served in Íseldur, made from the bark of the róabush

Saga Volsik – a former princess of Íseldur; she was seized by King Ivar and raised as his ward; she is betrothed to his son Prince Bjorn

Skald – a poet who composes a type of Urkan poetry, often exaggerating the deeds of kings past and present

Skarpling – a small, mouse-sized creature with quills on its back

Skjöld – a dried leaf taken to treat headaches

Skógungar – a forest walker; a peaceful tree-like creature that lives in the Western Woods

Slátrari – "the butcher"; a murderer who burns people from the inside out

Sólas – Íseldurian coin currency

Svalla Volsik – the former queen of Íseldur; she was murdered by King Ivar, her body impaled upon a pillar in the pits of Askaborg Castle

Stjarna – "mother of stars"; Sunnvald's wife and the goddess of weaving, fertility, and guidance; one of the old gods of Íseldur

Sudur – the southernmost territory of Íseldur; it houses the capital city

Sunnavík – the capital city of Íseldur, where Askaborg Castle is located

Sunnvald – the Sun God—king of the old gods of Íseldur; god of fire and might

Thrall – an enslaved person; in the kingdom of Íseldur they

are most often brought in from Norvaland and marked on their inner wrist

Urka – a large nation to the east of Íseldur where the line of Urkan Kings, including Ivar Ironheart, originated

Ursir – the Bear God worshipped by King Ivar and fellow Urkans; belief in Ursir has been imposed upon Íseldurians

Vampire deer – carnivorous deer that hunt mammals and drain their blood

Vestir – the westernmost territory of Íseldur; houses the Western Woods

Wolfspider – a large spider covered in shaggy gray fur

Zagadka – the mysterious island nation to the south of Íseldur

ACKNOWLEDGMENTS

Hekla's story was originally supposed to be in *Kingdom of Claw,* but given that it was already a long book, and this story felt like a side quest, it seemed better suited for its own novella.

It was so much fun getting into Hekla's head and writing such a badass warrior. But it's important to acknowledge that Hekla is this way because she's *had* to be in order to survive. I dream of a world where women don't need to wear armor. Where one-third of women haven't experienced intimate partner violence. Where women's rights aren't being actively stripped away.

If you are in need of help, see https://www.thehotline.org/ (US) or https://ccfwe.org/find-help-across-canada/ (Canada).

Special thanks go to my sensitivity readers GiannaMarie Dobson and Michelle Swinea, for ensuring that Hekla's disability and domestic violence background were portrayed in a realistic and respectful way.

Several books were helpful in writing *Roots of Darkness,* most notably *Finding the Mother Tree* by Suzanne Simard, *Entangled Life* by Merlin Sheldrake, and *Children of Ash and Elm* by Neil Price.

Thank you to my critique partners and beta readers for all your helpful comments and notes: Daniela A Mera, Elayna R Gallea, Maggie Cannon, Sasa Hawk, and Brittany Damazio.

Thank you to KD Guthauser at Story Wrappers for creating the gorgeous cover. Thank you to Friel at Grey Moth Editing for being an amazing cheerleader and editor all in one.

Thank you to Molly Thorp for your help in launching this novella into the world.

And as always, thanks to my family—to Z for bursting into my office, planting yourself on my chair, and stating, “I’m bored.” To K for bringing me your insanely creative Lego inventions. To B for never getting mad when I take the last cold Diet Coke and Coke, for watching *Survivor* with me, and for your endless support for this bizarre world I dreamed up.

Return to the Kingdom of Íseldur

in the Third book in the Ashen Series

DAWN OF THE NORTH

COMING WINTER 2026

Read on for a sneak peek!

PROLOGUE

Signe did not flinch as the High Gothi's dagger slid across the thrall's throat. A crimson trickle quickly grew to gushing, rhythmic throbs as the Gothi's acolytes rushed forward with cups to collect the girl's lifeblood. Signe watched the thrall's blue eyes go from wide and panicked to dull and unseeing as the low, undulating tones of the High Gothi's voice met her ears.

A hundred or so figures had gathered on the southernmost dock on this sullen, overcast day. Askaborg Castle loomed behind them, Sunnavík harbor's many piers stretching out before them. Gulls called overhead, the smell of seaweed so pungent it nearly overwhelmed the acrid scent of burnt corpse.

Nearly.

All morning, Signe's moods had wavered between disbelief and brutal, aching grief. It had to have been a mistake. The corpse in the ship docked at the end of the pier wasn't Yrsa. Surely her girl was just missing. Hiding perhaps. The chaos in the great hall had been so very frightening, after all. Any minute and her Yrsa would appear and reassure Signe that it had all been one big misunderstanding.

The High Gothi's voice shifted to guttural rhythmic

chanting as he poured the thrall's blood over the altar stone. Signe charted its course over the deep grooves carved into the stone; watched as it pooled in the trough below. When the thrall's lifeblood had drained from her, acolytes wrapped bear cloaks around her naked body before carrying her to the end of the pier and lowering her into the ship.

As Signe's gaze fell upon the figure in the center of the boat, tears tried to claw forth. The resplendent silks wrapped around the corpse could not hide the fact that the body was nothing but charred flesh and blackened bones.

Her baby.

Her Yrsa.

Signe's hand curled into a fist as she stared at what remained of Yrsa. Never again would she kiss her daughter's cheek. Never again would she hear the sounds of her laughter.

"Mama?" A small hand prodded her balled fist.

Signe forced herself to exhale and unclench her fingers, reaching for Hávar's hand.

"Not much longer, my darling," she said in a low voice.

Little Hávar had seen only three winters, and it was unlikely that he understood what was going on. In the days that had followed the explosion, he'd asked countless times for Yrsa, wrenching Signe's heart anew. But it was worse than merely her heart. It felt as though a piece had been torn from her very soul.

The next thrall was yanked forward, her ice-blond hair marking her as Norvalander. Beside Signe, Ivar loosed an impatient sigh. She ground her teeth together. *Get on with it,* that sigh seemed to say. *I've important matters to attend.* It was no secret that Ivar favored his sons above all else, but Signe had dared to hope he'd *pretend* to mourn his daughter.

Hávar's hand squeezed Signe's as the thrall girl wailed and thrashed before the High Gothi. Her elbow collided with one of the acolytes, sending the man staggering backward into an ornamental brazier. But the thrall's attempt to flee was fruitless; three more acolytes rushed forward and seized her. The High Gothi ended her with a slash of brutal efficiency, the wound on her neck opening like a crimson smile.

By the end of this service, five maidens would lie alongside Princess Yrsa to accompany her on the journey to Ursir's Sacred Forest. Signe hoped that the thralls and treasure heaped upon the ship were sufficient to allow her girl an afterlife without wanting for anything.

Her girl.

A sob broke low in Signe's throat, catching her by surprise. She turned away from the procession, trying to gather herself.

"Mother." The crackle of Bjorn's voice—not quite a man, yet no longer a boy—came from her right. He stood beyond Ivar but leaned behind his father to place something soft into her free palm.

Signe opened her hand and stared down at a clean square of linen. Such a thoughtful boy, her Bjorn had proven to be, and his kind gesture gave Signe the strength not to crumble.

She dabbed at a rogue tear, then faced forward once more. The latest thrall girl was lowered onto the ship, nestled between a bushel of apples and a cask of heather mead left over from Yrsa's birthday feast.

Ivar stepped forward, commanding the attention of all

those present. Clad in a fine red-and-gold tunic, her husband cut an imposing figure. Ivar might once have been the most handsome man Signe had ever seen, but now . . . now, half his face was a patchwork of oozing burns and peeling flesh, his once-striking beard singed short.

The beard, Signe knew, maddened her husband nearly as much as what he now dubbed the assassination attempt. The Urkans saw beards as a sign of male potency, and Ivar Ironheart's formerly chest-length beard was now so short, he could not even braid it. It was little solace to Signe on this day, though. Not with what came next.

The High Gothi passed an unlit torch to Ivar, who dipped it in the flames of a sacred brazier. With swift, efficient steps, Ivar strode to the end of the pier.

One more moment, Signe wanted to beg. *One more moment with my baby.*

But Ivar did not hesitate. He threw the torch onto the ship. Turned without ceremony.

Signe watched the flames catch—first on the hay padding the edges of the ship, then on the rich silks strewn throughout. The High Gothi cut the rope securing the boat to the pier, then worked with his acolytes to give the carved prow a gentle shove. The flames danced higher, higher, licking the skies.

Signe watched the boat drift away through a fog of tears.

But Ivar didn't see any of it. He strode past Signe. Put his hand on Bjorn's shoulder. "We have plans to make, son."

Ivar Ironheart left without watching the moment his only daughter departed the realm of the living.

Signe sat in an armchair arranged near the enormous glass windows of the king's bedchambers, a goblet of wine clutched in her hand. The clouds had lifted as the day progressed, and so Signe had ordered the room made dark so that she might gaze at the star-speckled skies. And as she stared listlessly up, she could have sworn one star blazed brighter before streaking amid the others. But as she blinked, it was gone, and with the amount of wine she'd already consumed, Signe couldn't be certain of much right now.

Her younger sister would have been able to name each constellation in the sky—would have been able to recite the Norvalander folklore stories behind them. Not a day went by when Signe didn't think of her, but here, now, her sister haunted her thoughts more than ever.

"I miss you," Signe murmured, then shook her head at the wasted emotion. She'd put her sister—had put all things Norvaland—behind her almost two decades ago.

Signe refilled her cup with an impatient breath. When would Ivar return from his meetings? All afternoon he'd been gone, busy preparing for retaliation against the Zagadkians. The fool of a man was convinced Kassandr Rurik had orchestrated the explosion in the great hall; that the Zagadkians had used the treaty as a ruse to gain access to Ivar and end his life. Had the man not seen Saga Volsik with his own eyes? Had he not known what the unnatural dark blue of her veins had meant?

Of course the dim-witted man did not. But Signe understood the significance of those veins—they meant that Saga Volsik had not acted alone. Because with them, in that room, Signe had sensed the presence of her old friend. Her secret friend. The one she'd grown to love and to trust over the years. Why had Signe's friend given themselves so wholly to Saga, when Signe had been so dutiful? And to kill her Yrsa . . . it was a betrayal so deep that it hurt her to even consider it.

Signe drank a large gulp of wine, forcing her mind back to Ivar and his foolish plans. He was adamant that Saga Volsik had acted with the Zagadkians, that she could not have done it alone. Saga was, as Ivar put it, "only a woman."

Her chest ached for what could never be. Yrsa's wedding to a high-ranking cousin of Ivar's. A quiet, safe life for her girl among the verdant fjords and rocky shores of Norvaland. Within a few short months, Yrsa would have been protected. Instead, she'd perished before Signe's very eyes.

Because of that ungrateful little *serpent.*

Signe swallowed a large mouthful of wine, desperate to dull the sharp pain of her grief.

Thankfully, the door to the bedchamber swung inward, diverting her attention. Ivar, it seemed, had finally returned. Signe set her cup aside and made to stand, but paused as a petite blond woman entered first. She recognized her at once as Eldrún, Ivar's favored concubine.

The queen's fingers curled around the arms of her chair as Ivar pushed Eldrún against the wall, groping her with the finesse of a drunken troll. Signe ought to have expected this—she hadn't, after all, warmed Ivar's bed in some time. But after Yrsa's funeral, such things had been far from her mind.

Clearly, it hadn't hindered *Ivar's* lechery. Anger burning

low in her stomach, Signe decided she'd seen enough. She stood and cleared her throat loudly.

Ivar whirled, his hand going to the sword belted at his hip.

"Signe." He exhaled in clear relief, but even in the dim light, she could see fear lingering in Ivar's brown eyes. Ever since the explosion, he'd grown paranoid that someone would make another attempt on his life. It would have amused Signe had it not come at the price of her daughter.

The queen's eyes fell upon Eldrún—scant years older than Yrsa. Her amusement quickly kindled into anger.

"Out."

The girl scampered away.

Ivar fetched a torch from the corridor, glancing at his wife in irritation as he used it to ignite the braziers in the room. Light danced along the walls and across the enormous carved bed that dominated the space. "I did not expect you to grace my bed tonight, Signe."

"And I," said Signe, "cannot fathom how you could take *anyone* to your bed the day your only daughter was sent to the Sacred Forest."

Ivar bristled as he slid the torch into a sconce. "What do you want, *wife*?"

Signe strolled toward her husband, his gaze hard and flat as he leaned against the wall.

Reaching him, Signe caressed his forearm with soft fingertips. Once she'd admired the toughened muscle of these arms. Once she'd admired *all* of her husband. Had desired him above all others. But the years together had hardened her tender heart. She forced herself to look past her husband's ruined face and meet his dark eyes.

"Vengeance, Ivar," she purred. "That is what I want."

Ivar pulled away, and though it shouldn't hurt after all these years, pain twinged in Signe's chest.

"You know I do not concern you with the affairs of men, Signe."

Ivar strolled to the table where Signe's unfinished jug of wine rested. Finding a goblet, he filled it, then turned to face her. And for the first time in *years,* Signe found traces of softness in her husband's gaze.

"But today, perhaps, I can make an exception. Will it ease your grief to know we plan to sail to Zagadka within a fortnight?"

A *fortnight.* Signe's mind raced. A fortnight was not enough time to muster all their forces nor for Ivar's father to arrive from Norvaland with his fleet. Fear twisted in her gut as she thought of Bjorn. She'd just lost a daughter. Signe could not lose her Little Bear, too.

"But your father's fleet—" With the winter ice floes between Íseldur and Norvaland, it would be some weeks before King Harald arrived. "Surely you can wait a little longer. With those numbers, you'll be unbeatable—"

"We *cannot* wait, Signe. The Zagadkian scum tried to assassinate me—"

"You do not know it was them," Signe interjected.

Ivar took a menacing step forward. "Do not interrupt me, wife."

Signe clamped her mouth shut, berating herself for reacting, as Ivar would say, *emotionally.* But when it came to her children, she'd always struggled to hold her tongue.

"You worry for Bjorn, that much is clear," said Ivar, coldly.

"Do you not know your worry weakens him in his men's eyes? He must see battle, Signe. Must sharpen his skills. Yes, this is happening sooner than we'd anticipated—"

"It is foolhardy!" The words burst from her before Signe could stop them.

Ivar's hand lashed out, slapping her hard across the face. Her vision exploded with white, burning pain, and Signe stumbled back, clutching her cheek. Ivar tossed his wine back in a solitary gulp, leveling a hard look at her.

"I warned you not to interrupt me, wife."

Signe forced her lips together. Forced herself to swallow the vile words trying to push up her throat.

"We sail two weeks from today. When my father's fleet arrives, they will join us. But I do not think we shall need them at all." Ivar's gaze grew distant and hungry. "We have some . . . battle innovations we are eager to use."

Signe's anger had grown to a living, breathing thing, and it took every ounce of her will not to release it on her husband. Instead, she focused it on the one person she despised above all others.

"I ask only one thing of you, husband." A deep breath eased her raging heart. Signe straightened her spine. Faced the beast of a man before her unflinchingly. "Bring Saga Volsik to me. Alive."

Ivar raised a quizzical brow.

Signe answered him with a queenly smile.

"I want to watch as the light fades from her eyes."

About the Author

DEMI WINTERS is the author of romantic fantasy books featuring softer female leads, grumpy heroes, and immersive worlds. Lover of all things fairy-tale, fantasy, and romance, Winters lives in British Columbia, Canada, with her husband and two kids. When she's not busy brainstorming fantastical worlds and morally gray love interests, she loves reading and cooking.

To keep up with her writing endeavors, join Demi's Crew in the Facebook group or newsletter or follow along on social media.

instagram.com/demiwinterswrites
tiktok.com/@demiwinterswrites